ADMIRAL TOM:

A SEQUEL TO

CAPTAIN TOM DRAKE;

OR, ENGLAND'S HEARTS OF OAK:

This splendid Sequel, by a talented Author, is written by the express desire of the readers of "Captain Tom Drake."

THREE NUMBERS COMPLETING THE WORK.

ADMIRAL TOM.

By the Author of "The Black Flag," "Tom True," "Will-o'-the-Wave," &c., &c.

CHAPTER CCXXXV.

THE DEATH TRAP—TOM DRAKE AND THE SCOUT BAFFLE THE INDIANS—THE FIGHT ON THE RIVER.

"Death!" how ominously the sound falls upon the ear, and even to the languid sufferer who has long looked upon life as a heavy burden. What terrible import it conveys.

Then how much greater must have been the effect upon one so young and active, so energetic, so aspiring, so hopeful, as was our gallant hero, Captain Tom Drake.

But it was not the actual fear of death that caused him to fall so prone and listless to the earth, far from it, for, as we have seen, he had fearlessly faced the grim monster a thousand times and in as many different shapes, therefore, it may be naturally asked, what occasioned his sudden collapse, when the five mysteriously glowing letters that formed the word "Death" shone out through the sombre darkness.

Weakened by the loss of blood, and still suffering acute pain from the wound where the bullet had grazed the side of his head, our hero had been seized with one of those presentiments, which is easily accounted for when the nervous system has by some unforeseen accident become suddenly deranged.

It was the shadow form, however—the image of his mother that worked so terrible an effect upon him.

It was her figure dressed as when he last saw her, but with pain-pinched face and quivering lips, from which the coldly-whispered word "Death" was emitted with vivid and startling distinctness.

Whether it was a spirit visit or only a phantasy, conjured up by his overwrought brain, Tom knew not, for, when brought to himself by the shock occasioned by the fall, he raised himself on his elbow, it was gone.

"Bah!" he muttered, as he sprang to his feet, and endeavoured to shake off the icy chill that permeated his brain. "I must banish these womanly qualms; have I not a mission to fulfil, a destiny to work out? Tom Drake must not yet talk, or even think of death."

The Scout was too much engrossed with his own thoughts to notice our hero's mutterings.

The hardy pilot of the flat boat had not seen the shadowy form, his keen eyes had been fixed on the gleaming letters of fire, which gradually faded and then died out.

"There's mischief brewing in that," he said, turning to Captain Tom. "Some treachery, or I am not born; but what it is I can't exactly make out yet."

"We had better keep strict watch, then," whispered our hero, who had now recovered his former self-possession, and was quite equal to the occasion, no matter how fraught it might be with danger. "There's no occasion to alarm the boys, let them sleep and rest."

This was agreed to, and the pair seating themselves on the ground watched for coming events, which they felt certain were portended in the mystic letters of fire.

And thus an hour passed, without a sound to break the monotonous and ominous stillness of the night air.

Even the breathing of Nature in the forest was hushed, and the low murmur of the gliding waters seemed to share in the silence of death.

At length the great round moon rose and flooded the forest and plain with its mellow radiance.

The haze which was so thick at the beginning of night soon faded away, and only that white vapour peculiar to Indian summer hung over the landscape.

This was a great relief to the silent watchers, especially to the old Scout, who now for the first time ventured to address our hero.

"Here's a queer go, friend, whatsomever your name may be," he said, in a gruff undertone, "I shan't mind when daylight comes, so that we can make a move."

Captain Tom was about to reply, but ere he could do so the old Scout sprang to his feet, as though some deadly reptile had stung him.

He gazed down at the ground where he had been seated with a strange and puzzled expression on his bronzed features.

"Ah, what is up?" queried Tom, in an undertone, and slightly perturbed at the strange and sudden movement of his companion.

"Darn me, if I couldn't a sworn I felt the sand move," replied the scout, in a tone only sufficiently loud to reach our hero's ears.

"A mud turtle," said Tom Drake; "they are common I should say about these parts."

The Scout made no reply, but having scrutinised the spot where the boatmen were coiled up in their blankets, he by main force lifted our hero to his feet, and dragged him some distance from the spot.

Tom could feel that the Scout's burly form was all of a quiver, and that his eyes blazed with excitement.

That something more than ordinary had disturbed him he felt assured.

"What is the matter?" Tom asked, "why you grip my arm like a vice, and——"

"Hush, I have made a discovery, snakes and scorpions are a fool to it. Did I not tell you I felt the sand move, but I did not tell you what I laid my hand on?"

"You did not. Was it anything alive?"

"It was. A red Ingin kivered up under the sand. I'll swear I caught a hold of his scalp-lock, and look you amongst those shrubs and clumps yonder, there's as many more as would take us an hour to count 'em."

Tom Drake scanned the spot pointed out to him, scarcely knowing what to think of the matter. At first he thought that the Scout, like himself, had been the victim of a delusion.

"How could they get there?" he said.

"We've been betrayed—that is, me and my bully boys, and there's a traitor amongst us as have put the Ingins up to our movements, and they've come here and buried themselves, so as to pounce upon us in our sleep, and like so many devils slaughter us to a man."

This was not cheering news for our hero, considering he had so recently joined the party.

Having partaken of their hospitality, he, however, determined to share their danger.

But there was another awkward difficulty to explain.

As he was a stranger to the boatmen, and had fallen in with them just on the eve of this dire calamity, might not suspicion point to him as the guilty party?

"I hope," he said, "that you have no doubt about my honesty, that I——"

"Fear not for that, stranger," replied the Scout, interrupting him. "If I thought you'd come here to sell us I'd shoot you. No, no, there's too much frankness in that face for me to suspect you; but, darn me, if I ken tell who's done it, and yet I can pick out a skunk by the look of his eye."

"Give me your hand, then," said Tom. "I detest treachery and hate a traitor, as you would know had we been longer acquainted. But how are you going to manage? I suppose their object is to get possession of the boat and its costly cargo."

"Just so, the thieving sarpints; but do you know they hate the white men for egsploring their rivers and trespassin' on their territory. Now, do you see? And that's how they lay wait for our scalps."

"Just so," returned Tom, who still kept his watchful gaze on the plain studded with clumps and shrubs.

"And what's tarnation wus," continued the Scout, clutching firmly his rifle, "I'd bet a sack full of dollars that unless we're out of this in less than a jiffy they'll rise up like a host of demons and wipe us all out."

Tom did not hear this announcement without a slight feeling of uneasiness.

He thought of his mother, of Minnie, of his brave followers, and he liked not the idea of being "wiped out," as the old Scout described it, without having the chance of ever seeing them again.

To have fought on the deck of his noble ship against any unequal number would only have been to him a pleasure, but to be scalped and slaughtered, perhaps tortured by a host of bloodthirsty fiends, who lay burrowed like so many reptiles under the ground, was not at all consistent with his feelings.

He was not at all superstitious, but he now could not help thinking that some terrible disaster was foreshadowed by the appearance of the death lights.

And his mother's form, too, appearing to him at that time. There was something in that he could not make out.

Was she dead, or was she in danger, and now praying for his timely succour to rescue her from some terrible fate?

Little did he dream what she was enduring at that moment.

It would have driven him mad, had he known that she was confined in the dark, fetid hold of a Moorish pirate galley.

Then he thought of Minnie, and his brain whirled when he considered the helplessness of his situation.

These thoughts flitted through his mind in a moment.

"What's to be done?" he at length said, as his restless soul began to chafe at the Scout's inactivity.

"Well, I'll tell ye," replied his companion, whose thoughts, in spite of his silence, had been working hard all the time. "There are two canoes on the flat boat. They must be launched, and when we get them quietly afloat, we must rouse the boys and take our hook like a greasy streak of lightning."

"Can we do this without raising suspicion?"

"We must try for it. They're on the watch, those red devils, and we must go as crafty as snakes about our work."

"Good," said Tom, who felt relieved at the prospect of doing something. "We can't stay here to be butchered and——"

"It's agin my grit, too, stranger," said the Scout, between his grinding teeth. "This way. Come softly, and keep a smart eye on anything that moves."

Once on board the flat boat the canoes were soon slid from off the deck; and then, leaving our hero to keep watch over them, and to give notice of any suspicious movement amongst the shrubs, the Scout went and aroused his sleeping friends with a tact that could only be practised by one who had learned it by well-earned experience.

During this time, nevertheless, several pairs of dark, piercing eyes were watching their every movement; and whilst the Scout was informing his friends of the terrible danger that menaced them, and that they must fly in the canoes and leave the flat boat behind, the plain in the direction pointed out by the Scout as the suspected ground, began suddenly to upheave with a motion of a rolling sea. From the shrubs and bushes dark forms sprang up like scores of reeds, and then, with a whirling motion, shook the sand from off them in showers like ocean spray.

There was no need for secrecy now.

Cunning eyes had watched every movement of our hero and the Scout.

Why the savages had remained in that quiescent state so long was a mystery to Tom.

This was explained when the Scout gave a startling cry and caused all eyes to wander across the river.

On the opposite bank, floating high up, as it seemed, in the hazy mist, was the strange and terrible warning of death, that Tom and the Scout had previously witnessed, only somewhat robbed of its radiance by the presence of the moon, and this was evidently the signal for attack.

The dread letters, however, were plain enough to strike terror to the unsophisticated boatmen, who, as they uttered the werd "Death!" clutched up their rifles and scrambled into the canoes.

"Steady—steady!" thundered the Scout, and Tom, with his usual forethought, warned each one to look well to the loading and priming of his weapon.

Fortunately for them the savages did not swoop down upon the white men at once. They had some mystic rite to perform, and a sort of war dance to go through, which was to ensure them a certain victory.

As the canoes were being gradually slid off the sloping bank, four men in each were told off to work the paddles, and then with a steady "Yeo ho!" the fragile and overloaded canoes were shot rapidly into the stream.

With a wild whoop the savages now rent the air.

In one dark mass, like a shower of locusts, they swooped down towards the beach.

Halting there, they then poised their spears

aloft, and those who had rifles prepared to take steady aim at their retreating foes.

"Down—down, darn ye!" thundered the Scout, and his men, acting on the warning, had only bare time to stoop down and avoid the murderous shower.

"Well done," cried Tom Drake, "well done. Now, lads, give the red devils a check."

Then the rifles of the white men rang out, causing a diversion on the shore, and several dark forms were seen to fall close to the water's edge.

Captain Tom was in his glory just then.

The rifle, which had been given to him by the Scout, was a weapon of which any good marksman might be proud; and Tom had used it with unerring effect, for his bullet had dashed out the brains of one of the foremost warriors, and shattered the jaw of another one in his rear.

The Scout, however, seemed to have lost all power and energy for the moment.

He had, in fact, just discovered that old Dan was not among them.

He could not even remember his joining them when they so hurriedly embarked in the canoes.

As Dan was a very good swimmer the Scout ignored the idea of his having fallen overboard in the scurry and being drowned. Then why this sudden and mysterious disappearance? And at such a moment, too. On the face of it it looked suspicious, and in his own mind the Scout readily conjectured that he was the traitor who had sold them. But he kept his thoughts to himself for the present. He had other thoughts to occupy his mind just then.

The Indians had evidently made up their minds to wade into the stream after them.

This was apparent by the fact that several of them had stepped into the river, and were sounding its depth by the aid of their long, slender spears.

The Scout had, for his own particular reason, not called his men's attention to the absence of old Dan, but at this critical juncture, when the Indians were preparing to dash into the river and engage them hand to hand, an accident happened which threw the boatmen into a state of dire confusion. A ridge of sand, hidden by the water, arrested the progress of the canoes, and upon it they stuck hard and fast.

Of this sad occurrence the bloodthirsty savages took immediate advantage.

Having no time to use their rifles, the Indians, brandishing their spears and tomahawks above their heads, rushed wildly into the stream, and, being only knee-deep in the water when they reached the sand-bank, they surrounded the canoes, and waged a terrible warfare with their occupants. Clubbing their rifles, the white men stubbornly maintained the fight, standing back to back, and scattering blood and brains in all directions.

Captain Tom had now a good opportunity of displaying his exquisite skill.

Having broken his rifle short off by the stock in smashing in the skull of a gigantic red-skinned warrior, he seized the Indian's spear and used it as a boarding-pike.

Several of the boatmen, however, had by this time succumbed to the unequal contest, and many more brave hearts would doubtless have shared the same fate, only that the tide rose, floated the canoes, and thus changed the tide of battle in the white man's favour.

Goaded to desperation, the savages then strove madly to drag the canoes back to the shore again, but the tide gaining in swiftness, and Tom Drake dealing death and disorder around him, baffled them in this object.

Strangely enough, although the water rose, the stream continued to run like a race horse down towards the sea, an undercurrent setting upwards causing the river to rise so that when the canoes were free they glided rapidly clear of the sand bank.

The red-skin demons, nevertheless, exerted their utmost to annihilate their foes, even when the water reached up to their necks they, with their tomahawks and spears, battered away at the canoes, determined in this manner to sink them.

It was in defending the bow of his canoe that young Harry lost his life, a blow from a long-handled tomahawk cleft his head in two, which so enraged the Scout that he raised his rifle to his shoulder and shot the red skin through the skull.

At this juncture a reinforcement put off from the shore.

They had stayed behind considering their presence would not be needed, and indulged their thieving propensities by taking possession of the flat boat, and removing from her whatever they could plunder.

To plunge into the river and swim to the aid of their worsted comrades, was but the work of a few minutes, and the air resounded with their yells as they watched several dark bodies being borne down the rapid stream, their arms lashing the water into foam, in their convulsive throes.

In this manner, and with the fight still fiercely waging, the canoes were borne a mile or more down the stream, the savage horde being terribly thinned, and only four of the white men, besides Tom Drake, remaining, all of whom were bleeding profusely from their wounds.

Wearied with their exertions and almost dying of thirst, the brave whites began almost to despair of holding their own much longer, for those in the river continually harassed them by swimming under water and coming up close to the canoes, thus prodded them unawares, and was away again beneath the surface out of sight before they inflicted upon the savages any injury.

Added to this, a dozen or more of the dusky fiends followed them along on the banks of the shore, and hurled at them great stones, cocoanuts, and other missiles that chanced to come to hand.

Captain Tom and the Scout had but small opportunity to hold a palaver or council of war.

In fact their throats were so parched and their lips so shrivelled that they could scarcely articulate a word.

That this state of affairs could not continue much longer, they both knew full well, but two such indomitable spirits were not likely to give in while strength enough remained to them to keep the red skins from capturing the canoes.

A spear thrust in the thigh soon after disabled the Scout; but, as he sank down into the bottom of the canoe, he had the satisfaction of seeing his crafty adversary seized by a huge cayman, or alligator, and borne down beneath the blood-stained water out of sight.

The canoes were now drifting past the opening of a lagoon, under the spreading trees of which that lined its banks; a dozen or more of the hideous scaly monsters were lazily looking about them and sniffing the blood-scented air.

As a couple of these four-footed cannibals glided from a muddy nook in the bank, and with steaming nostrils swam swiftly into the stream, the Indian with affrighted yells, and terror-distorted visages made for the opposite shore, and thus ceased hostilities.

Rid of one ruthless enemy the palefaces now had as bad or even a worse set to contend with.

The alligators, whose numbers momentarily increased, made straight for the canoes, and, with open mouths and clashing jaws, prepared to attack the wounded occupants.

This new danger was enough to crush the hopes of the wounded whites, and, were it possible, would have wrung tears from the monsters themselves had they been similarly placed.

Captain Tom Drake was quite equal to the occasion, however.

That the cayman would endeavour to capsize their frail craft, or make daring attempts to drag the occupants out into the water, he was well aware. Therefore he called to the rest to reload their rifles, and to try their skill in putting a ball in the eye of each monster as it approached.

As an example Captain Tom lodged a bullet in the left eye of the first one that came up, and the Scout did the same favour for its companion.

The other three men contented themselves in watching when the insiduous animals opened their massive jaws, when they fired into the huge cavity, which was a target that no ordinary marksman could well miss.

Another difficulty then arose.

The ammunition was nearly run out.

Just one charge each man was all that remained.

As a last extremity these were collected and divided between Tom and the Scout.

Four shots was all they now had to depend upon, and then they would have to fight the monsters at close quarters for bare life.

CHAPTER CCXXXVI.

THE TRIAL OF EBONY—ADRIFT ON THE OCEAN—TERRIBLE SUFFERINGS OF MRS. DRAKE AND JENNY VERE ON BOARD THE CORSAIR CRUISER.

THE wind was light, the bright sun shone on the blue and sparkling sea, upon which the good ship "Spitfire" sat as gracefully and almost as motionless as a sea bird, when the boatswain's pipe rang out, and his hoarse voice summoned all hands to muster on the quarterdeck.

Then silence again reigned.

No sound was echoed save the patter of hasty feet, the rattle of a block or the creak of the cordage as the ship gave an occasional roll in the long, smooth swell of the sea.

A drum-head court-martial was about to be held, and the culprit to be tried was no other than Ebony, the black cook, who was accused of the crime of having laid the train of gunpowder which was to set fire to the magazine, and blow the vessel, with all in her, into the air.

How this dastardly and inhuman intention was frustrated our readers already know, so that we have no need to recapitulate it here.

When the crew mustered, and those who were to act as judges had taken their places, the culprit, looking ghastly in the extreme, was brought up from below, and with his arms pinioned, he, between two seamen with drawn cutlasses, was led into the poop.

There was a sinister gleam in his restless and quailing eye as he passed between the ranks of his shipmates, whose stern looks and scowling glances showed that they had no pity for the ruthless wretch.

Harry Vere, Bob Hauler, and Jerry Mizzen conducted the court-martial.

Minnie Atherton was also on deck, but only to hear the evidence and watch the proceedings.

The trial itself was merely a formal one; the case rested purely on circumstantial evidence, but this was so conclusive that it was impossible for the judges to arrive at any other decision than that the accused was guilty.

There were no extenuating circumstances even, for what could be more horrible or more detestable than such an attempt, though the excuse might have been made that it was prompted by revenge. Therefore the sailors assembled were desired to consider the sentence, which they pronounced as in the voice of one man—

"Death! death! death!"

Minnie shuddered, and the culprit staggered as if he had been shot.

His dusky visage changed to a livid green, and his guilty soul shrank within him like parchment when subjected to the heat.

When silence was restored, Harry Vere, who had before addressed the men, again spoke.

"Are you all unanimous in this? Is there no dissentient?"

"None. Death! death!" was the stern but solemn reply.

There was a dead pause.

The hard breathing of the guilt-stricken and cowardly wretch was plainly audible.

His bloodshot orbs rolled in agony as he watched the faces of the resolute men.

He could read no pity there, but he could see the horny hands clench as though anxious to grasp the rope that was to run him up to the yardarm.

Suddenly a cry broke the painful stillness.

It was Minnie's, and all ears were attention then.

"If there is none here who will show him mercy, let me, at least, plead for him," she said.

Then with moistened eye and streaming hair she sprang between Harry and the excited seamen.

Harry Vere drew back in submission before her.

Then, with a deferential bow, he said—

"Speak, lady; we all have an ear for your supplication."

"Then spare his life, I pray—nay, I implore you."

"For why—why?" murmured several of the men.

"That he may live to repent," she answered, pleadingly.

There were none to gainsay this.

No matter what they thought to the contrary, not one had the courage to express it.

Her word, her very look was law, even to those hardy toilers on the ocean.

For the affianced bride of Captain Tom Drake there was not one of the crew, saving the wretch for whom she interceded, but would have laid down his life.

"Then his life is to be spared," said Harry Vere, after a long and painful pause. "But, as a security of our own lives, he must not remain on board. Lower a boat!"

This was done.

A pair of oars, a mast and sail, were then

thrown in, and a keg of water, with a small bag of biscuits, was placed in the stern.

The culprit was then ordered to the gangway, where his arms were unpinioned, and he was fastened under the arms to the end of the rope which was already rove for sending him a journey into the air.

By its aid he was lowered into the boat; the rope was then cut, the boat's painter was cast off, and the boat, with its solitary voyager, drifted away from the ship.

The guilt-laden wretch then recovered his former possession.

With wild glaring eyes, and a fierce tigerish expression, he glared at the seamen as though he would have liked to have torn the heart out of each one separately.

Then, having uttered a string of the most vile and insulting invectives, he gave a shriek of derisive scorn, and hoisted his little sail.

Gradually, gradually the ship and the boat parted company; but as long as they kept in sight of each other Ebony still kept up his horrible menaces.

And even as the solitary speck dwindled away into nothingness the howling of the maddened wretch could be heard above the moaning of the sea.

Not until it was lost to sight did the sailors, who had watched its slow recedence, again breath freely.

Soon after the soft breeze sprang up into a gale.

The tall masts of the "Spitfire" quivered and bent, and the sails bellied out to what portended to be a storm.

But all hearts on board her were lightsome now. They had ridden the ship of that black plague spot which might have consigned them to an untimely doom.

Yet other dangers awaited them, and one in particular of which, had they had but the slightest inkling, would have made their very souls recoil with horror.

*　*　*　*　*　*　*

Let us now change the scene to that inland sea, the Mediterranean—the home of the Moorish rover, and the hunting-ground of the piratical Algerines.

About five leagues distant from the African shore, to which she was heading, though almost becalmed, lay the Corsair vessel, in the hold of which Captain Jordan, of the ill-fated "Clara Jane," and the female captives were incarcerated.

The captain was in irons, heavy manacles encircled his wrists, and around his waist was a stout band of iron, to which was attached a brace of chain shot.

The two ladies were placed apart from him, but in a no less uncomfortable spot, for not a ray of daylight was allowed to beam upon them, so that they were doomed to linger in one incessant night.

Had they but a friendly voice to cheer them it would have ameliorated their sufferings, but no living soul did they hear or see, only at such times as their grim and pittiless gaoler brought them their food.

And thus a week passed.

A week of the most excruciating torture, both to mind and body, when one morning Jenny Vere was awakened from a troubled dream with a start, and found Mrs. Drake raving like a maniac.

"Unhand me, miscreants, it is my darling boy;

let me fly to his assistance, do you not see that the scaly monsters are tearing him limb from limb, devouring his tender flesh, mangling his heroic form—and—and—"

Jenny Vere sprang up from the pile of soiled velveted cushions, which the Corsair mockingly had provided them with for a bed, and by the dim light of the smoky lamp, discovered Mrs. Drake upon her knees with her hands frantically clasped, and her pallid features bathed in cold and clammy sweat.

"What—what is the matter?" exclaimed Jenny, in a tremulous voice, her own frame still trembling with excitement, occasioned by a dream she had had of her husband.

Mrs. Drake glared at her with wild and vacant eyes.

"I have dreamt of him, my son, Tom Drake," was the widow's hysterical reply; "I saw him a captive in the land of Egypt, a prisoner in the house of bondage; I beheld him dragged before my eyes down to the banks of the River Nile, where his noble, his dearly cherished form, was mangled by the scaly monsters of the worshiped river."

Jenny Vere shuddered and gave a start.

"Eaten by crocodiles," she mechanically said.

"Aye, 'tis true. I saw it—I saw it. Oh! my brave, dear boy. Why did I allow you to ever leave me? Why did we not die together?"

The brave girl knelt down beside her, and, having bathed her hands and face in cold water, strove to comfort her.

"Calm yourself, dear madam," she implored, her clear silvery voice sounding like music in that dismal hold, "I too have had a dream—one of hope. I saw my dear Harry bounding on his good ship to our rescue, and I saw him slay our cruel tyrant at my feet."

"Alas! alas!" moaned Mrs. Drake, who, like Rachael, refused to be comforted. "It is to good to be true. Did you not read my son's letter in which he desired me to meet him at Gibralter. May he not have been taken prisoner like ourselves, sold into slavery amongst the Egyptians, and—ah, what's that?"

Mrs. Drake shook like an aspen when she gave utterance to this startled explanation.

Above them they could hear the Corsair captain shouting in his native tongue.

Then followed a clattering of hasty feet, ropes were thrown down with a hollow clang upon the deck, various orders were hoarsely bawled through the brazen speaking trumpet, and then the heavy creaking yards were hauled round, and the flackering canvas shook the vessel from truck to keel.

All this occupied but a moment.

Then the pale listeners knew by the dull swash of the sea against the vessel's sides that the ship's way was stopped.

Then there were preparations as of some one of importance being ushered on board, and soon after Jenny recognised the voice of the much-dreaded Hassan. Soon after the hatch above them was raised, and a gaudily dressed Corsair descended into the hold.

"Come on deck, senoritas," he said, in a strange mixture of broken English and Spanish, "Rais Hassan, the admiral of our fleet, desires your presence."

Mrs. Drake nearly fainted.

Jenny Vere felt a convulsive shudder pass through her frame.

But it was gone in a moment, the brave heroine had, by her wonderful instinctiveness, mastered the qualm, and prepared herself for the ordeal she so much dreaded, and yet was aware she must go through.

Rais Hassan was the oldest admiral in the Corsair fleet. His long, flowing beard of a slightly yellow tint gave him a patriarchial and fatherly appearance, although, in Jenny's opinion, it seemed to have become rusty and discoloured with iniquity and age.

He was magnificently attired.

His sumptuous dress was elaborately trimmed with gold and silver lace, and was decked with costly jewels, which shone and blazed with various coloured hues at every turn and motion he made.

The crafty old sinner had well studied the weakness of the gentler sex.

He had donned this exquisite and dazzling raiment to blind and daze the sense of the lovely English girl who had promised to become his bride.

Had Jenny been a weak-minded girl, she might easily have fallen into the trap.

But her brave, true heart was her Harry's. She was already a sailor's bride, and her heart was as true to her marriage now as the needle to the pole.

Therefore she saw through his deceit at once; but having learnt by bitter experience to treat craft with craft, she pretended to be amiable, at the same time maintaining her own modesty and reserve.

The Rais, now confident of success, gazed on her in rapture, for the carnation tint, produced by excitement and indignation, gave her that loveliness which no artificial means could have produced.

To be brief, the interview was completed in the magnificently-appointed cabin, where Jenny consented to redeem her promise on one condition.

She had to make an untruthful prevarication to accomplish this.

She said that her father had gone down in the ill-fated ship, and as it was through the Corsair captain's own act that her parent had thus ruthlessly lost his life, he must allow her three months at least to mourn her loss, and to prepare herself for her new situation.

To this Rais Hassan was at first averse, but after a deal of argument, and a moderate share of reflection, he yielded.

Jenny placed no great reliance in his promise. She doubted not that he meant to deceive her, and would most likely use violence towards her before that time expired.

Yet she trusted in providence and the innocence of her own heart to protect her; and, having whispered a few consoling words to her grief-stricken and still weeping companion, she pretended to cheerfully comply with the Corsair chief's request, which was that they should be removed at once to his own galley.

This was a change for the better—in one sense, at least.

There they had female slaves to wait upon them, and everything, saving liberty, that they desired.

Mrs. Drake was astounded, and although she could not still the secret fluttering at her heart she, by Jenny's advice, assumed an appearance of resignation and cheerfulness.

The brave girl, having once entered upon the path of deceit, was now compelled to follow it up step by step, which she did in a manner astounding to herself.

She even condescended so far as to wear the dress of a Corsair maiden, and studied so as to be able to converse with the Rais in his native tongue, and so worked upon his credulity as to actually induce him to consent to her reducing his long flowing beard, dyeing it, and making such alterations in his appearance as made him look much younger.

And yet for all this her young heart was sighing. And many a time and oft she breathed a silent prayer as she vainly gazed out of the cabin-window, and scanned the dark blue rippling ocean in the hope of descrying a friendly sail.

Thus day after day came and went, until she felt within herself that she could not bear the agonising suspense much longer, whilst the dreaded hour was drawing near, and the presence of the pirate chief grew at each meeting more detestable.

CHAPTER CCXXXVII.

ADMIRAL ELLIS IN TROUBLE AGAIN—CAPTAIN TOM HAS A NARROW SQUEAK OF HIS LIFE.

WHILST Tom Drake and his staunch adherents were thus actively engaged in a distant clime, no news of Tom's whereabouts reached the authorities at home.

By some he was almost forgotten in the excitement occasioned by the approaching war between England and France, for the press-gang was actively at work, and the dockyards were in full swing, fitting out their fleets to meet England's inveterate foe.

At the "Blue Lobster," however, his name was frequently mentioned, for amongst the smuggling fraternity that assembled there, the visit of our hero to the coast of France was freely discussed.

His being cast into prison, his daring escape from the fortress, and the horrible death by which it was supposed Black Bill had expiated his crime, were all known to them and in other quarters too, as the Government at that time employed a great number of men in their secret service.

But such doings could not remain long in obscurity.

What was known at the "Blue Lobster," soon found its way into the *Gazette*, and all England rang with the name of the famous Tom Drake.

Farmer Inglis was delighted with the news. He rubbed his hands and chuckled inwardly, for he hoped that one day Captain Tom Drake would pay another friendly visit to the farm-house.

In aristocratic quarters the excitement was equally intense.

In the leading newspapers of the period the daring achievements of our hero were fully reported and commented upon.

In the seaports and offices connected with the Admiralty the doings of the redoutable buccaneer chief was all the talk, and many of the grey-headed, old sea veterans praised our young naval hero for having outwitted Old England's inveterate enemy, the French.

Reuben Harpy and his colleagues were, of course, all the other way—to have heard of his death would have been joy to them.

They therefore formed a sort of secret league against our hero, amongst the members of which were conspicuous Admiral Lord Kilcrew, Lord Augustus Vane, and the Commodore and Admiral Ellis.

There were a host of others, which it is needless to name. They were friends of those we have mentioned, and had not only influence at court, but they also had friends and relations holding appointments under Government.

It was through their recommendation that Admiral Ellis had his vessel revictualled and an extra complement of hands put on board, and received a commission to cruise about the French coast, with his Britannic Majesty's warrant to sink, burn, or capture the daring "Boy Rover," Captain Tom Drake.

To have successfully accomplished either of these feats would of course have been not only the making of the vindictive little admiral, but also the greatest pleasure he could have dwelt upon for the remainder of his life.

He even went so far as to give a grand dinner during the necessary equipment of his ship, to which the chief members of the league were honoured with an invitation.

But the admiral's impulsive nature and deadly enmity towards Captain Tom led him once more to commit a most serious error.

Having arrived off the French coast one night, he, in the darkness, came close upon a vessel, a brig, and this, in his narrow-minded judgment, he concluded at once was the "Will-o'-the-Wisp."

To disable her of course was his first object, and he commenced at once to beat to quarters, and fire upon her.

Soon after, to his dismay, he discovered by accident that the vessel he had so hot-headedly been pounding away at was a despatch vessel, bearing a Government official, with private despatches from the French Government to that of the British Admiralty.

From that day no tidings of Captain Tom Drake, his brave buccaneers, or of his "Will-o'-the-Wisp" little vessel, reached England, and in the quarrel between the two nations, which was urged forward by the stupid and un-Englishlike conduct of Admiral Ellis, the brave little crew were almost forgotten.

At length war was proclaimed, hostilities commenced, and time flew on so rapidly that it brings us again to our story, and we here remind our readers that the missive purported to come from Captain Tom Drake to his mother was kept secret, as was also the departure of Mrs. Drake and Jenny Vere, and likewise their intended destination.

That the latter was written in a feigned hand, and was the work of an astute villain, an enemy to the noble boy captain and his friends, the reader has already doubtless surmised, but of this hereafter we cannot diverge, but proceed on the even tenour of our story.

* * * * *

In a beautifully secluded spot overlooking the sea three men halted and rested their load under the shadow of a tall palm tree, and then paused to get breath.

Although scarcely recognisable owing to their scratched, blood-stained, and muddy appearance, they were no less important personages than the Scout, and the only two survivors of the flat boatmen.

The burden they had rested had been borne between them on a rudely-constructed litter, upon which reclined a human form, covered over with broad leaves to shield it from the sun.

"Snakes and thunder, Sam, it was warm work up that hill; he's small compared to me, but deuced heavy. I wonder whether he'll live after the great service he's done us, or whether

he'll croak, and leave us all in mystery as to his name, and where he came from, and so forth."

"I hope he'll pull through," answered the man addressed. "He's a pluck 'un, whoever he is; but I hear the ripple of water. Run, Jack," turning to the third man, "and bring us some here as quick as you can, lad."

"Aye, aye," Jack replied, and having selected a couple of big coocoanut shells, plenty of which strewed the ground, he darted off.

"Yes, he's a pluck 'un," Sam continued. "Tarnation thunders, what havoc he played with those caymen; they'd have eaten us up sure enough if he hadn't a used that knife as he did."

The Scout was about to reply, but at that moment a commotion in one of the dense clumps of flowering bushes startled him.

"Look out, Sam," he had barely time to gasp, when a man forced his way through the foliage, followed by others to the number of a dozen or more, all armed to the teeth.

"Hallo, have you seen a black looking nigger pass this way?" said the foremost of the party, addressing the Scout, as with rapid strides the new comer approached him.

"I aiv not," answered the Scout, eyeing him suspiciously up and down. "We have had enough of the dusky devils, if it's anything like a red Injin that you mean."

"No, its a nigger I want," said the man, "as black as old Belzebub, and twice as crafty; he's about here some where, and I mean to unearth him, or my name's not Hugh Baldrick."

As the latter spoke his eye rested on the litter, and fancying that he saw the leaves move, his suspicion was aroused that the negro was concealed there.

Accordingly he strode towards it, and throwing aside the leaves with a careless hand, a discovered a prone form swathed in blood-stained bandages.

Then he gave a start.

"Shiver me—heaven protect us; why, its Captain Tom," he exclaimed, in his bluff, but kindly seaman-like manner.

"Captain Tom," echoed his friends, who by this time had gathered around, "Captain Tom, what, our dearly-beloved Captain Drake?"

"Just so, and a pretty pickle he is in, hang my toplights, there's been foul play at work here. Who are you?" he added, turning fiercely upon the astonished Scout.

A few words of explanation then ensued, which providentially prevented more blood being shed, by which time Jack appeared with the water.

Seizing one of the vessels from his hand Hugh Baldrick then knelt down, and tearing the kerchief from his neck he dipped it in the water, and, having wiped the blood and mire from our hero's face, he moistened his lips with a little brandy which he poured from his flask.

In a few seconds his unremitting attentions were rewarded, and Captain Tom Drake, to the intense delight of all, opened his eyes and gazed upon the sad visage of Hugh Baldrick, and the anxious faces of his boy buccaneers.

It was some time, however, before our hero was sufficiently strong to sit up, he could talk though, and that was some consolation.

As he lay thus prone, Hugh Baldrick answered him many questions, and one of all others that endowed the young chieftain with new life, and enabled him to sit up with his back rested against the tree.

"Yes," continued Hugh Baldrick, "Minnie

Atherton, I can assure you, is safe. As we were combing the beach in search of any vestige we were likely to discover of yourself, we fell across a miserable object in a shattered boat which had gone ashore in the night and been dashed upon the rocks."

"Oh!" echoed Tom, deeply interested.

"His yarn was that he was one of the crew of the 'Spitfire,' commanded by Harry Vere, and he mentioned the names of Ben Barnacle, Jerry Mizzen, and a lot of others, whom he said had raised a conspiracy to get him hung."

"Yes. Well, well."

"And he would have been hung, too, according to his yarn, if his life had not been spared through the intercession of Minnie Atherton."

"Ah!" ejaculated Tom, springing to his feet, "she is safe, then; but where is the 'Spitfire' now? Whither was she bound?" he inquired excitedly.

"That the nigger couldn't tell; he was set adrift in a boat, and got wrecked, as I before said.

"And his crime?" said Tom.

"That he didn't state; some rascally work, I should say by the devilish look of his figure-head—but here comes the fellow; let him answer for himself."

Captain Tom, and, in fact, all present, turned their eyes towards the spot indicated, and beheld the negro being dragged along by Ben Barnacle and another fellow, whom the Scout immediately recognised as his runaway skipper. Old Dan was being led between two other buccaneers.

On beholding the latter, the Scout became mad with fury.

But before an arm could stay him, or those present could even divine his purpose, he leaped forward with the spring of a tiger and felled the old skipper to the earth.

"Back, back! this is my quarrel," thundered the Scout, as several of the buccaneers rushed forward to seize him. "He betrayed me to the Death Indians, caused me to lose my boat and a valuable cargo, besides a good jorum of gold, the fruits of the hard labour and savings of myself and my crew. Curse him, the sarpint! And he is the cause of your captain, Tom Drake there, being in the awful state you now find him," he added, pointing to Tom's blood-stained bandaged form—a home thrust which, as may be supposed, went straight to the hearts of the young buccaneers.

Leaving the Scout, therefore, to transact his own business the buccaneers clustered round the black, and their threatening gestures warned him not to play with them, but answer each question truthfully.

It took a deal of cross questioning, however, to draw from him what they wanted, but when they had elicited all that they could depend upon as facts they allowed him to depart, with the understanding that he was never to cross their path again, unless he desired to be flayed alive.

Captain Tom was an altered being when he knew that his Minnie was in safe hands.

"I feel strong enough to walk now," he said. "Let us away to our ships, and embark at once."

But his brave buccaneers would not hear of this. They placed him again on the litter, and, hoisting him shoulder high, allowed him barely time to shake hands and take leave of the Scout and his companion Jack, when they hurried him away in great triumph.

CHAPTER CCXXXVIII.

HOW TOM DRAKE BECAME AN ADMIRAL — THE GREAT SEA EMERALD FALLS INTO THE HANDS OF ADMIRAL TOM.

THE return of Captain Tom Drake was hailed with joyful acclamation by his followers.

"Hurrah! hurrah! hurrah!" was shouted from every lusty throat, and echoed back by those on board the ships to whom the glad news had been at once conveyed by signal.

"Hurrah! hurrah!" was uttered by the feeble lips of the sick. "Thank God! if I die now I shall die happy."

Zelie was no less excited than the rest.

The lovely Corsair maiden sprang on deck as the first outcry was raised, and, seizing a powerful spyglass, eyed with rapturous glance her wounded idol, the princely boy.

At this juncture Dutch Paul sprang to land, and elbowing a passage through the group of excited middies clustered round their chief, he seized the hand of Captain Tom, and grasped it warmly.

"Welcome back, my brave boy," said the princely Paul with much fervour. "What to us would have been this victory had it cost you your previous life? Of what worth would be the costly treasures—the mass of wealth we have secured—were you not here to share it with us?"

"Thanks, generous friend," replied Tom, his eyes sparkling with their wonted brilliance.

"Thank you, I thank you all, for this proof of your unselfish devotion to one who can only repay you by offering you the services of my still strong right arm, and the knowledge I have gained by my hard-bought experience."

"Hurrah, hurrah, Captain Tom, hurrah! Three cheers for our Buccaneer King! Hurrah, hurrah, hurrah!"

Three shouts coming from stentorian lungs made the shores ring again, and sent the echoes vibrating among the distant hills and surrounding rocks, whilst from the ships they were answered by salvos from their loud mouthed cannon.

King George could not have had a more regal welcome had he returned to England with a victorious fleet, nor could he have had a greater proof of loyalty than was expressed in the honest grip and fervent handshaking that our hero had to go through with his brave allies, his officers, and his delighted followers.

It was some time before these joyful ebullitions subsided.

In fact Hugh Baldrick had to use more than gentle force to press back the elated boy buccaneers before he could get the young captain away to a place where he could arrange his toilet, and partake of some much-needed refreshment.

Whilst thus engaged the stalwart Iron Arm strode into the siege-battered room, and, grasping our hero's hand, he shook it warmly, while a silent teardrop glistened in his eye.

"Tom," he said, his strong voice faltering with suppressed emotion, "I am proud to find you in this honourable and glorious position. Although it is not more than I expected of you, and I pity that country which drove one, so noble and generous, from its shores, and thereby deprived itself of the great services, you could have rendered it had you still served under its flag."

Tom Drake, with the modesty of a true-born

hero, bowed his head in acknowledgment of Iron Arm's speech.

"Gentlemen and brother adventurers," he said, "I know you will excuse me making a long speech. It was not to war with these Spanish miscreants that I especially came here, it was to wrest from the power of a merciless pirate, one whose virtuous honour was at stake, and one whom you all know I love dearer than my life."

"Hear, hear, proceed brave Captain Tom."

Our hero bowed again, and then, mastering the tremour that shook his voice, continued—

"News has reached me that she is now under the protection of one of our illustrious and trusty friends, Lieutenant Vere, who, for what we know, may be still hovering upon the coast, perhaps in some danger, as he is now in an old and patched-up ship; therefore it is my bounden duty to leave this scene of carnage, and fly to their succour, even though I should have to scour the sea from pole to pole."

Ben Barnacle, who had filled the silver goblets with sparkling Spanish wine, and was all aglow with excitement, waiting to speak, now burst out in stentorian tones—

"Bravo, Captain Tom! Here's a health to the rover's queen, Minnie Atherton, and to her bold and gallant sweetheart, admired Tom."

A hearty laugh went round at this, then the toast was drunk amid the chink and rattle of the massive silver goblets, until the oak-panelled walls and the fine old ceiling rang again.

Dutch Paul, who sat at the head of the board, then addressed the company—

"Gentlemen, buccaneers, or rovers," he said, whilst a smile sparkled in his large, bold eye, "our old friend, Ben Barnacle, has, by his able and eloquent speech, furnished me with a suggestion, which I will put to you and I hope you will all approve of."

"Name it—name it!" shouted Hugh Baldrick.

"It is that as his Britannic Majesty, King George, has so many admirals in his fleet who are in reality no more fitted for the rank than the grimiest powder monkey (Admiral Ellis I may name as one), and who has never gained a victory worth recording, why should not our gallant Tom Drake be raised from the rank of captain to that of admiral?"

"Why not—why not?" thundered Barnacle, rising, excitedly, and thumping his horny hand upon the table. "For no cause whatsoever. Let him be admiral, gentlemen all, say I, and let his name resound as such from sea to sea, so that when our grandchildren and our great, great grandchildren, if we should have any, grow up they may read the daring deeds of Admiral Tom Drake, and strive to emulate them."

This honest and John Blunt style of speech drew forth a thunder of applause, which was joined in by a score or so of Tom's buccaneer crew, who were carousing in an adjoining chamber, and had heard all the foregoing conversation, owing to a shot rent in the wall that divided the two apartments.

At this juncture a most important personage made her appearance.

It was Zelie.

The beautiful Arabian girl had been seized with an unquenchable desire to be once more near, and to stand again in the presence of the proud boy chief.

She had heard with exceeding joy that Minnie was away on the sea, in an old ship with Harry Vere, and she wished the whole lot, even Bob and Jerry, might go into the briny depth, and find a resting-place in the coral caves that abound in those tropical seas.

It was Doctor Shrike and his shadow, Jacop, who had told her this.

Under what pretext she managed to get on shore at this particular moment we shall now learn.

Tom, who really doted on her as he would a sister, returned the glance she gave him with equal ardour, and then, having placed his arm round her voluptuous form and imprinted a kiss upon her olive cheek, he inquired what brought her uninvited to that assembly.

"Behold, and judge for yourself, noble captain," was the girl's sweet reply; and she pointed to Jacop, who had entered the room unnoticed, and now stood with both arms encumbered with the case that contained Tom's beautiful uniform coat, with its splendid gold epaulettes, the tin case in which was his best gold-laced cocked hat, and his dress sword with the magnificently-jewelled hilt.

Tom was delighted, and expressed his approval by kissing her other cheek, then, having gently released the blushing girl, he donned his hat and coat, buckled on his sword, and then he underwent the ceremony by which he was rated admiral.

"Now," said Hugh Baldrick, "if there is any one present who can show any just cause why Tom Drake, owner and commander of the gallant 'Will-o'-the-Wisp,' should not be proclaimed Admiral of the Seas, let him speak, or for ever hold his peace."

No one spoke.

There was a general silence, when Ben Barnacle, unable to restrain himself any longer, blurted out—

"There's not one who dare do, and if there was I'd fell him with this 'ere flipper, and knock seven bells out of his carcase with the same ease as a horse would kick him."

The middies, who had collected at the door, and had been watching the proceedings in excitement, now rushed into the room in a body, and, clashing the blades of their swords and dirks together so as to raise a din, gave three ear-splitting cheers for Admiral Tom.

By this time the news had got wind and had flown from mouth to mouth, so that everyone knew, even those on board the ships, that Tom Drake had been honoured with the title of Admiral, and a royal salute of minute guns was fired from the three stately vessels.

Gaily coloured bunting was also profuse, and an extra jorum of grog was of course indulged in by the jolly Jack tars.

Having thanked Zelie for her kind and thoughtful consideration, Admiral Tom hinted his desire to return on board, but Dutch Paul prevailed upon him to accompany him over the ruins, so as to assure himself that the work of demolition was complete.

As they proceeded the gentleman smuggler gave him a rough estimate of the treasure which had been secured in strong iron bound chests, and equally distributed among the ships.

"And now," he said to our hero, when the latter had expressed his satisfaction, and they had concluded their examination of the dismantled fortress and its battlements, "I have one more thing of importance to show you."

As he spoke they were passing the door of a little chapel, and leading the way into its gloomy interior, Dutch Paul pointed to a bier on which was laid a body covered carefully with a pall.

Tom gave an involuntary start on beholding that well-known covering of the dead.

It was his own flag, the black banner with its horizontal red stripes that Bob Hauler had so hastily prepared when they played such havoc among the Algerian pirate fleet under the withering fire of their own blazing forts.

As Paul raised the sombre emblem, and revealed the corpse beneath it, all present gave an inward shrug, for the features had been battered out of recognisable shape, but the limbs and body were encased in a suit corresponding exactly with the attire worn by Tom during the desperate conflict with the Spaniards.

In a moment Admiral Tom mastered his emotion.

"What means this insult?" he hoarsely asked, as the fire flashed indignantly from his eyes. "Speak, Paul. I command you, and end this mummery at once."

Dutch Paul answered him very coolly.

"Avast!" he said. "This is no mummery, Admiral Tom, on my part. This is the cunning work of the treacherous Spaniards, the piratical scoundrels dressed up this youth, to represent you so that he might appear at one of the embrasures, and bid us cease firing, perhaps order us to retire; and in the confusion, we believing it to be you, the pirates might thus have deceived us, and have thereby gained an advantage by which they might have rallied their forces, and there is no knowing what mischief to us it might have done."

"Ah, I see it all now. Pardon my haste, trusty Paul, but how came he by this horrible death."

"In executing his treacherous object of course. He was killed by a falling beam, and we found his disfigured corpse among the ruins. Believing it to be yours, and no wonder as you were missing, and the face was so crushed and disfigured. I had it secretly conveyed here so as not to cause an alarm to our men."

"Very thoughtful of you, and very well arranged, Paul. You could not have done better under the circumstances, but thank Providence the traitor has met with his reward, and I am here to prove to you how just was that swift retribution."

"At the same time," added the admiral, venturing a cynical smile, "you might have spared me the pain of seeing my proud flag so misused, and yourself the trouble of sending aboard my ship to obtain it for such a purpose."

"Splice my timbers," cried Ben. "The land crab aint got half his desarts. I would have liked to clap flippers on him, and to have scorched his skin with the cat afore he squared up his reckoning on earth."

"I forgive him," said Tom. "Let him be decently buried, it is the fortune of war, and he must have been a brave fellow to have dared to impersonate me."

Admiral Tom Drake was now all anxiety to get away.

His mission to the pirate isle had so far been fulfilled, but he had not yet succeeded in his main object in paying a visit to those seas. To up anchor and set sail in search of the "Spitfire" was now his earnest desire, and with all speed he made his way on board, accompanied by Ben Barnacle who had secured the much coveted flag.

That night there was great rejoicing aboard the ships, and at early morning they weighed anchor and set sail, each taking a different course to go in search of Harry Vere's ship.

Tom Drake, when fairly under sail, kept a look-out at each mast-head, mounting himself at times to the crosstrees to scan the shore and the horizon with his glass, when some object he sighted caused him to alter the "Will-o'-the-Wisp's" course, and run into a little bay.

His ship was then hove to, a boat lowered, and as soon as she was rowed to the beach he sprang ashore, and strode rapidly towards the strange scene he had witnessed from aloft.

It was two lifeless bodies dangling in the breeze, suspended by the necks to the branches of two opposite trees.

Distorted as were the features of each he soon recognised them both.

In one ghastly visage he saw that of the black, Ebony, and in the other the face of Old Dan, the flat-boatman.

"Well, well," said Ben Barnacle, who had kept pace with his chief, "how matters twist about of themselves. Split my wind if all things don't come round as easy as boxing the compass, and they go to their last account, one after the other, like the pawls of a windlass."

"So they do, Ben. This is evidently the work of the Scout. I believe he was a thorough true-hearted fellow, and if we could fall in with him, I'd recompense him for his kindness to me."

As an earnest of this, Tom and Ben ascended to the rising grounds that topped the trees, and having looked about with no avail, they descended to the boat and returned on board.

Tom then continued his search right round the island, entering every bight and bay where it was at all likely a ship might at anchor lay hidden, and then falling in with the other ships, he directed them which course to steer.

Having dipped flags to each other, and fired a parting salute, Dutch Paul steered to the southward, Hugh Baldrick due east, while the "Will-o'-the-Wisp," under easy sail, skimmed along towards the islands that are clustered about the mouth of the Florida Gulph.

With two restless spirits on board, such as Tom Drake and the invicible Iron Arm, the crew of the buccaneer ship had a lively time of it.

Not a sail, not a speck on the ocean escaped observation, and every vessel they overhauled, even to the tiniest sugar drogher, was hailed and closely questioned.

In this the middies heartily joined, for they were all anxious to get a glimpse once more of their old friends Bob and Jerry, whose cheerful visages were often missed, especially when the larks and pranks were carried on in the dog watches.

At length, one morning as Admiral Tom and Iron Arm were pacing the quarter-deck in conversation, a cry from the mastheadman brought all hands on deck.

"A black object, sir, in a strange-looking thing, no bigger nor a mother Carey's chicken," was the sailor's way of describing it, in answer to Admiral Tom's quick hail.

Tom Drake snatched the glass Ben handed to him, and sprang aloft like a cat.

"It is a strange object," he said, as, jambing his back against the masthead to steady himself, he surveyed what appeared to be a drifting boat with the sail lowered, and in its place at the masthead something hoisted in its stead.

On altering the ship's course this object was observed more closely, and as the "Will-o'-the-Wisp" sped nearer to it, Tom was enabled to make out that the object at the masthead was a man.

"Heave too! drop the gig," then he shouted, and then he ran down from aloft to see that the order was promptly and properly obeyed.

This, we may add, was scarcely needed, for every soul was on the alert, even Doctor Shrike, who gave Jacop a slap on the ear with his scalpel for not appearing at his elbow with his case of instruments at the moment he wriggled his thin, snake-like form up the ladder.

Before the impetuous speed of the smart little vessel could be stopped the gig touched the water, was unhooked from the tackles, and was sent cleaving the waves in the direction of the castaway boat.

"Good Neptune!" exclaimed Ben Barnacle, as the boats grated each other's sides and he looked up at the mast, which, rocking to and fro, swung the object in the fashion of a pendulum, "the fellow is hooked up, and hanging by his belt. How could he have got there?"

"I can see plain enough," said the young buccanneer, who grasped the gunwale of the boat to keep the gig's bow to, "the becket on the sail-yard is broken, and——"

"Ah! I see. Dash my lamps," cried old Ben, "he's been sitting on the yard watching us, no doubt. When the strop gives way, down comes the sail and yard, and the hook of the halyards just catches his belt."

"That's it," said another of the mids. "It's hooked him behind, and, of course, there was no chance of extricating himself, and there he's swung, doubled up like a V upside down, until all the wind's gone out of him, and now he's as dead as a rope-yarn, I daresay."

Ben Barnacle had by this time cleared away the halyards, which were lying entangled in the bottom of the castaway boat, and, throwing off the hitches from the belaying-pin, lowered the man down.

"He's not quite dead," said one of the two middies who caught him in their arms. "Let's hurry aboard, there's just a bare chance of saving him yet."

Once on board his surmise proved correct.

When the usual remedies had been applied, and he showed signs of returning life, Doctor Shrike took him under his charge, below, and had him placed in a cot.

"What a splendid subject for my museum, Jacop," he said, as that worthy held the dish preparatory to the doctor's usual bleeding; "and such a head, too, with the bumps of craftiness, avarice, and greed fully developed."

Admiral Tom had crept so softly down the ladder that the old vampire had no idea he was listening to him.

The noise, too, made by the trimming of the yards as the vessel was again put on her proper course, served to deaden the sound of the admiral's footsteps.

Stepping back into the shade cast by the shadow of the hatchway ladder, Admiral Tom watched the doctor's skilful manipulation of the lancet, at the first sharp probe of which the sailor gave a spasmodic start, and wresting his arm free from the hands that held it, clutched at something hidden in his breast.

But the bloodthirsty Shrike captured the arm again, and with a snake-like hiss gave it to Jacop to hold, but the man, as if seized with a sudden delirium, rose up in the cot, and seized the vampire by the throat.

A short but desperate struggle then ensued, in which the cot was so violently swayed from side to side that the occupant was pitched out, and fell like a sack of sand upon the doctor's attenuated form, under which was the body and appendages of the miserable and unfortunate assistant.

Alarmed at this, Admiral Tom flew at once to the rescue, and having raised the prone form of the man and placed him again in the cot, he beheld, to his horror, that the long stiletto-like probe which the doctor had used was buried to the hilt in the chest of the unfortunate castaway.

In his descent he must have fallen upon it, and that, too, very forcibly, as it required some strength to remove it, which accomplished, our hero tore open the breast of the injured man's shirt to examine the wound.

In doing so he discovered that the man wore round his neck a stout silken band, to which was attached a small leather bag, which lay on the chest of the seaman in such close proximity to the wound that the admiral was compelled to remove it.

As he did so he became aware that it contained some hard uneven substance, not at all like a miniature—the image of some dear and distant one, but something of such a peculiar formation that Tom Drake gave a start

What could it be?

He felt it again.

Then he passed his fingers over the angular protuberances, and a strange light kindled in his eye.

"Yes, it must be—it is," he thought; "the shape—the size—both answer to the description, and I—I—must have it, even if it carry with it that terrible curse which rumour has so hideously ascribed to it."

So strong was the impulse upon him that Admiral Tom felt the object again, and the contact not only caused his finger ends to tingle but produced a sensation in them just as though he had placed his hand in a cauldron of liquid ore.

All this only occupied a few seconds during which Tom concluded he had discovered the famous sea emerald, and he stood like one dazed, entranced, as it were, with that inward knowledge that the precious and much-coveted treasure lay there within his grasp, and yet he had not the power to take it.

Suddenly a shudder passed through the man's frame.

He tossed his arms wildly about him, and seemed to wrestle with some one in the air.

Admiral Tom watched him in a state of feverish excitement.

"Was this his death throe?" he thought, "or was the suffering wretch returning once more to consciousness."

As though in answer to our hero's thoughts the man entwined his long, bony fingers round the bag, and opening his eyes fixed their cold glassy stare upon the face of our hero.

So searching was that glance that Admiral Tom feared the man would divine his inmost thoughts, and guilt-stricken, he shrank back from him with consciousness of fear.

Strangely enough, only one single drop of blood has oozed from the wound, and this puzzled Tom, although if he had possessed the power to reason he would have known that the man was inwardly bleeding to death.

DOWN, DOWN HEADFOREMOST CAME POOR HARRY VERE.

Presently the pain-parched lips of the sufferer began to move, and Shrike, who by this time had recovered from his undignified position, moistened them with a sponge, which enabled the sufferer to articulate—

"Tom—ah—Tom Drake, I know you," gasped the man, "and as I feel that my time grows short, my cable of life is veered out, thankful am I that this hour of atonement is come."

Admiral Tom, who had been expecting the man would denounce him, stook like one suddenly transformed to marble.

"Who are you?" he asked, failing to recognise the features.

"Peter, the Spy, the tool of Sanderson, the plaything of your bitterest enemy, Admiral Ellis, and the discarded tool of that consumate villain, your cousin, Rueben Harpy."

Admiral Tom was his former self again.

His dark eye lit with its usual fire, and the hot blood thrilled through his veins.

"Then you know the Blue Lobster and the Yellow Vulture," said the young admiral, controlling his rising passion with a mighty effort.

"Both, and Captain Angel, too, whom I often made secret assignations with at both places. It was he, the pirate, the scoundrel, who set me adrift in that boat many days ago."

"What had you done to displease such a good master, for by your own admission you are not the honestest of rogues?"

"I kept him apprised of your movements, laid your tracks down to him as plain as the marks and deeps on a lead line, but because I would not reveal a secret which would have supplied him with money enough to fit out a formidable fleet with which he could have scoured the seas in search of you. I, with several others who have plotted and yielded to bribery for the avowed purpose of encompassing your overthrow, were condemned to a lingering death."

"What became of the others?"

"They died," answered the castaway, sullenly, averting his eyes from Tom's penetrating gaze.

"Through starvation I suppose? They—they became food for——"

"The sharks," echoed the man, hastily.

"So I should say. The red stains in the boat, and those dull-looking patches on your clothes denote as much. But what was this secret?"

"Nothing, nothing," exclaimed the man, who seized with the instinct of clinging to life whilst a single chance remained, clasped his hands over the bag as if to conceal it.

This act set Tom's mind all of a whirl.

That the priceless gem for possession of which men had schemed and plotted, and even parted with their very existence, was imprisoned in that greasy bag he had now not the slightest doubt, and as a wild delirium seized him, he grappled with the dying man, and they both struggled frantically for its possession.

Both Shrike and Jacop, awe stricken, gazed on the scene, although it was but of short duration.

The weaker gave way to the strong, the ribbon parted, and as Admiral Tom almost frenzied by the touch of the mystic talisman, tore it from the hands of the dying sailor, the castaway fell back and expired.

Having secured it Tom's heart throbbed with wild and tumultuous joy.

Without even deigning a look at it he placed it hurriedly in the breast of his rover's jacket, and strode up the ladder on deck.

As he passed Iron Arm, who was leaning against the bulwork talking to Barnacle, he endeavoured to look calm, but both noted the wildness of his eye, although they attributed it to a far different cause; and then down into the cabin Tom went, his mind swaying between joy and fear; for did he not possess the great green sea emerald, which would make him the envy of the world; and had he not hastened a guilty wretch into eternity a few seconds earlier than was ordained.

Such were his conflicting thoughts, as he hastened into his state cabin to feast his eyes on the glittering bauble, so that it might light up his soul with its dazzling brilliancy as it had lighted up the souls of others.

Oh fatal, fatal gem, how mysteriously your magic power is working.

CHAPTER CCXXXIX.

CAPTAIN ANGEL BOARDS THE 'SPITFIRE'—MINNIE ATHERTON'S TRIUMPH.

THE storm that had so long been foreshadowing at length burst with relentless fury on Harry Vere's ship, and the wind howled and shrieked its wild requiem to the black inky waves as sail after sail was rolled up or reefed, until the "Spitfire" was but a little better than a vessel scudding under bare poles.

She steered wildly, too, through the maddening waves that boiled up on either side of her, and rose towering astern with a terrible roar, threatening to poop her and sweep her decks of every living soul.

And through that dreary night, lit up occasionally by the lightning's vivid glare, which only served to render the darkness more intense.

Harry Vere kept his post at the quivering wheel, for he thought of the peerless treasure that through fate was confided to his care, and only occasionally did he leave his post to visit the cabin and whisper to Minnie Atherton a comforting word.

For three days the storm raged with ceaseless fury, and during that space the gallant "Spitfire" had ploughed league after league of the white capped seas, when the wind suddenly moderated, the bright sun shone out, and then Harry found that they had been driven among the islands that abound on the African coast.

This was not pleasant, not at all calculated to cheer and invigorate the young watch-worn commander, nor those whose fatiguing exertions had almost prostrated them.

In their pleasant plight with an old ship, and an armament exceptionally small, if the Corsairs should fall in with them, they would have tight work to hold their own, and to prevent Minnie Atherton falling into the hands of the merciless wretches.

To make matters worse the wind died down to a calm, the "Spitfire" lay motionless as a log upon the glaring ocean, and the water in the casks was running short.

Taking advantage, however, of the fine weather, Harry Vere used all possible speed to put his vessel in trim and repair the damage sustained in the gale, so as to be ready when the breeze again came.

He took the precautions also to have the sails brought up from the store-room, so that they might be thoroughly repaired.

It was thus all hands were busy, when the cry of Jerry Mizzen, who was engaged aloft, apprised them that a sail was in sight.

Bob Hauler had just opened his glass previous to taking his survey of the horizon, and as Harry replied to the startling cry, he snatched the glass from the hands of old Bob, and he sprang like a cat up aloft.

Scarcely was he two minutes absent when he was down again on deck, and looking Bob straight in the face, he said—

"She's a heavy ship, too, carrying royals and sky-sails, and she's carrying a wind that I'd give a fortune for just now."

"Oh," said Bob, as he cast a furtive glance across the waters, "I can see her now, she grows apace, too, and as she's heading straight this way. I'd wager my can of grog she'll be down on us afore another hour glass is run."

And Bob Hauler's surmise was correct.

The strange sail sped so fast before the gale that her snowy canvas rose up from the rim of the horizon and expanded like a cloud, each moment growing larger and more distinct.

Then her tall hull appeared, and as she drew nearer Jerry Mizzen tumbled down from aloft, and, looking as pallid as a ghost, rushed on to the quarter-deck.

"Oh, lord!" he said, "Mr. Vere, Captain Angel's aboard that craft!"

"Captain Angel!" exclaimed both Harry and Bob Hauler in a breath.

"Aye; I seed him standing right forard like, in the eyes of her. Look! look! d'ye see that face within a line with the figger'ead?"

Harry Vere raised his glass, and took a long survey, whilst Micky, the marine, who kept sentry over the companion door, sprung his ramrod, and then, inserting it into the barrel of his musket, rammed the charge well home.

Micky delighted in fighting, although he was such a coward when shipwrecked. He kept casting vicious glances at the oncoming ship, and longed, if there was any fighting to be done, for her to get within range of his bonny brown Bessie.

"Confound it!" cried Harry Vere, suddenly, as he lowered his glass and closed it with a vicious snap. "Confound it!" and he stamped his foot heavily on the deck.

And by his sudden manner the trio gazed at him in askance, not one of them daring to ask him what he thought.

"Captain Angel it is, and in that big ship, too," he exclaimed. "Prepare for action; we must not let that demon set his foot on board of us."

There was a commotion at once among Harry Vere's small but trusty crew.

The name of Captain Angel worked quite an electrical effect upon them now they were certain of his presence.

When they were enabled to get a glimpse of his repulsive visage from the deck as he glared at them over the bulwarks, they gave vent to oaths, and would have given him a broadside at once had not Harry restrained them.

It was the young captain's desire to learn Captain Angel's intention before he threw away powder and shot, and he hoped in the meantime that the breeze the tall pirate ship was carrying would reach his own sails, and thus render the "Spitfire" fit for handling.

He had not long to wait.

The speed of the pirate ship was tremendous, and even in less time than Harry had calculated upon she leaped alongside, and the "Spitfire" was grappled fore and aft just as the breeze caught her light canvas up aloft.

Captain Angel then, armed with a pistol and brandishing a broad-bladed cutlass above his head, sprang on to the bulwarks and gave one of his demoniacal peals of laughter.

"Aha! a merry morning to you all," he thundered. "I suppose I have paid you this visit unexpectedly?

"Oh!" he added, as a bullet from Bob Hauler's pistol grazed his whiskers, "I will soon show you how to play such games better than that."

With this he sprang like a tiger on to the "Spitfire's" deck, and Harry, cutlass in hand, resisted with desperate energy his terrible onslaught.

As the captain made the leap, a score or more of his black-hearted crew threw themselves over the bulwarks on to the "Spitfire's" deck, whilst others, creeping out of the ports, reinforced them. Then five or six of the boarding party, who were attired as officers, urged them on with shouts, intermingled with threats and imprecations, to what bid fair to end in terrible slaughter.

Bob Hauler, with a chosen few, supported Harry against the unequal number that menaced him on the quarter-deck; and Jerry Missen led the main body of the "Spitfire's" crew against the blood-thirsty horde, who, mingled with the "Spitfire's" crew, now formed a surging mass of struggling beings between the waist and the vessel's bow.

Strangely enough, not one big gun had been discharged as yet, but this was easily accounted for.

Captain Angel preferred to carry out his nefarious practices as quietly as possible.

The boom of a gun might bring down upon him some of the Sallee Rovers, who would only be too eager to share his quarry with him, and perhaps wrest it from him altogether.

He had plenty of hands on board to work the guns if he so chose; but when he found that the fight was likely to be a tough one, he gave the signal for them to also board the "Spitfire" and join in the fray.

Harry was at this time bleeding from several severe scratches, and also hotly opposed; but, for all that, he ventured to cast his eye towards the party now leaping aboard, and among them easily detected Reuben Harpy, whose sallow visage was now changed to a livid green.

Brave as he was, young Harry could not repress a groan when he saw his case so hopeless.

Outnumbered, five to one, he could conceive nothing but annihilation before him.

Jerry Missen was wounded, and forward of the deck his men were, more than half of them, cut down and bleeding, and being trampled under foot by the fierce contenders.

It was easy to see that the pirates were gaining the mastery, and even Bob Hauler, who had been in many such a fix before, began to despair.

When he saw his young leader felled by the butt-end of a musket, and Captain Angel standing over him, he gave vent to a groan of pent-up agony, and the next moment he was himself stretched to all appearance lifeless on the deck.

The battle was virtually over now.

Captain Angel grinned like a hyena, and showed his fang-like teeth.

"Ha! ha!" he laughed, turning to those around him, "this is his ship, bear him aloft, and lash him to the topgallant masthead as a signal, and a warning to others."

Reuben Harpy gave a ghastly grin.

"That's business, Angel," he said exultingly. "I wish I had my dear cousin, Captain Tom Drake, here to send up aloft also, that he might decorate the other mast, and keep him company."

There was a loud, brutal shout raised at this. A series of hoarse guffaws, such as could only emanate from the throats of such a pack of hungry wolves.

In the meantime Captain Angel descended to the cabin.

"A—ah, empty, by Jove!" he exclaimed, as he found no one there, and no occupant in either of the state cabins.

"Stay," he added, as he espied something protruding from the chink of one of the coverings of the after lockers, "this looks like a portion of feminine bunting; let me overhaul."

To throw aside the velveted cushion that covered the locker was his first act, and, then dashing open the lid, he thrust in his sword, and soon felt that it met with some sort of resistance.

A slight pressure then brought forth a stifled cry, then a shriek, and in less time than we record it the brutal captain had thrust his arms into the dark cavity and brought out Minnie Atherton.

"Oh, my beauty, my essence of loveliness!" he said, in a tone of mocking suavity. "My jewel, how came you here? So you have forgotten your petted Tom, the boy pirate, and taken up with his discarded lieutenant, eh, my sweet one?"

Minnie Atherton, who was about to swoon, suddenly fired up at these goading taunts.

"My Tom," she said, "I am true to still,

and were he here at this moment your foul tongue would not utter such words again. 'Sdeath! how is it you have so long escaped perdition?"

Captain Angel bit his lips.

He could scarcely check his rising wrath, but, with the low cunning of his brutal nature, he forced a sarcastic smile, and replied to her.

"Let me embrace you, whilst, like the busy bee, I kiss the honey from these sweet lips."

"Never! Why are you here?"

"Simply, my adored one, because I love you, dote on you, for is it not wisely ordained that cherubs should dwell in the society of angels."

Minnie Atherton regarded him with a look of ineffable scorn.

Drawing her queenly form haughtily erect she said boldly—

"Reptile, were oh, were I a man I would crush such a cringing worm under my foot. Cowardly dastard, I spurn you."

Having worked herself up to that pitch of vehemence, she struck him with her silken-slippered foot, an act that Captain Angel never for a moment suspected she was capable of doing.

It took him so by surprise that for some seconds he stood in bewilderment, until his blind passion gave way to hatred, and he half drew his sword to menace her.

But the young girl did not flinch, neither did she evince signs of fear; her defiant attitude set off her peerless form to great advantage; so much so as to fill the black heart of her persecutor with jealous envy.

"Put back your sword," then she said, "the affianced bride of Tom Drake has no fear of death; as a proof I have here the means to protect my honour, or to resent any farther outrage you may so disgrace your manhood to attempt."

Captain Angel was not used to look tamely on and listen to such words as these.

The fiend who could cut a hundred throats in cold blooded sport, and tear the innocent babe from its mother breast, and hurl it into the sea.

Therefore he hissed as he bared his glittering teeth—

"Madam, my love for you is too pure for me to harm you. I will ween you to me by my endearing caresses, and then——"

The deep boom of a loud mouthed cannon startled him at that moment and checked his utterance.

"What is that?" he thundered, his flashing eyes starting almost from his head.

"Captain Angel! Captain Angel!" cried the squeaking voice of Reuben Harpy down the companion hatchway.

Then, with a string of fiercely-muttered expletives, the pirate captain turned and left the cabin and sprang upon deck.

But the sight he saw was not one that was likely to please him; the "Spitfire" and her captor were both becalmed, and just within shot range was a large felucca flying the rover's red flag.

"Curse them, may a thousand curses light on them for interrupting us just at this time," shrieked Captain Angel, tearing wildly at his fierce moustache.

"Lieutenant Harpy, why did you not inform me of their presence sooner? Now, how can we return the fire of their guns, becalmed here too, unable to move, but at the sport and

mercy of the currents, which reduces us to the strait of a rat when caught in his hole."

This was true.

The rovers, no matter of what nationality, whether from Greece or Barbary, could play havoc with the two motionless ships with their long brass cannon.

CHAPTER CCXL.

A STRANGE MEETING ON THE LONE ISLAND—SANDERSON HEARS UNPLEASANT NEWS CONCERNING ADMIRAL TOM.

IT was on one of the many islands in the Caribbean Sea that Mrs. Harpy and old John Gregory, two very important actors in our story, sat on a grassy mound overlooking the bay, conversing upon topics that cannot fail to be interesting to our readers.

It was evident they had not long met on that distant shore, and that they had been brought there at separate times by the Death Pirate, who, like a hungry hawk, was continually pouncing down upon some poor waif of the sea, but for what object he brought them there, the story itself must disclose.

"Oh, John Gregory, how glad I am that we have met. I thought they had driven you mad that you were dead, and that I was doomed to pine and die here in solitude without again seeing one familiar face."

"And how strange it is that we should thus meet!" said old Gregory, thoughtfully.

"It seems incredible. Who could have foretold such an occurrence? None but Dame Shipton, had she lived in our time, John. No one could else could have predicted our meeting here on this awfully lonesome land."

"Land, well, it is land," said old John, surlily; "but it's an island, and I have no doubt the deeds of our misspent lives have brought us both here. Mine has, I know, for had I not threatened to send my dear nephew, Tom Drake, to sea, I would always have had a protector, and you and your son would never have been able to have so played into the hands of that villainous Sanderson as you have done."

The widow gave a deep sob.

"Don't taunt me, John," she said, tearfully; "I have suffered enough for my misdeeds. Have I not been persecuted by the man I allowed to take possession of my heart. He not only, I must tell you, mocked me with a false marriage, and——"

"It was your own fault. In your weak moments you yielded to the voice of the tempter."

"I know it—I know it, John, and I was the cause of my injured husband leaving his native land and going I know not whither."

"Indeed," exclaimed Gregory, in surprise. "Was he not drowned, as it was supposed, when he mur—— I mean when he caused the death of my brother-in-law, Tom Drake's father?"

"He was not," replied his companion, rocking herself to and fro; "nor was Tom's father murdered. He went away, too, and all through the villainous Sanderson, whose machinations were working his ruin. But I wish I was once more home in England, for I know much, and I have a presentiment that Tom Drake will, after all, turn up in the flesh and wreak that vengeance upon Sanderson that his evil deeds justly deserve."

"All too late, you—we shall never leave this island alive. The Death Pirate, that terrible being who brought me here in his ship, gave me too full assurance of that."

Mrs. Harpy shuddered.

"The Death Pirate, that hideous monster with a fleshless mask," she said, "did he bring you here, John, as he did me."

"He did. He discovered me floating on a plank at sea, but as the circumstances attending my being there serves only to harrow my feelings when I revert to them, I beg you will be silent upon that subject for the present."

"I will endeavour to comply with your request," said Mrs. Harpy, with a sigh. "But tell me one thing, did he know you were related, or in any way connected, with Tom Drake."

"He knew all, he told me so. I learnt from him that he hated my nephew, who had braved his power on the deep, had hoarded the terrible pirate, Mrs. Harpy, and had almost succeeded in tearing the ghastly visor from his face."

"Then we are lost," Mrs. Harpy moaned.

"He learnt from me my changed feelings towards your brave nephew, Tom Drake, and he vowed to wreak his vengeance on all and every one who entertained one spark of sympathy towards the noble boy."

"And depend upon it he will, Mrs. Harpy. The power at his command is so immense, that I may describe it as grandly awful. From what I observed, when a prisoner on board his ship, I should say he was in league with the powers of darkness."

Old John's voice now grew so feeble and thick, that he arose and refreshed himself at the little stream that ran purling by at their feet before he spoke again.

Then he said in a much firmer tone—

"Mrs. Harpy, since we are doomed to dwell together on this island, let us, at least, bury all the animosity of the past. The pirate left me plenty of food, and my hut is large enough for both to dwell in, why not——"

"Nay," she answered him, quickly, "I would rather dwell alone. I will meet you here at at any time you choose, John, but the hours of my solitude I must spend in prayer—prayer to Him above who alone can give me aid and comfort in this hour of trial, and send some good ship to bear me away to my distant home."

"May your entreaties be answered," said Old John Gregory, as he reverently uncovered his head. "I will meet you here in the cool of the evening, and we will then discourse further on the subject. I have much to tell you that seriously concerns the interest of my nephew, Tom Drake."

* * * * *

Turn we now to the family mansion of the Atherton's.

In one of the best rooms the villainous Sanderson sat alone, a prey to the most devouring thoughts, a misery to himself, and a dark cloud to the servitors he had about him.

The night was cold, but the heavy curtains were closely drawn across the windows, and a bright fire blazed upon the hearth, yet there was a coldness in the apartment that sent a chill through its solitary occupant, and, in spite of all the comforts that surrounded him, rendered the guilty wretch both nervous and unhappy.

And well might he be so.

Dark mysteries hung around the ancestral hall. Every chair seemed to be filled with some misty occupant, the paintings on the panels of the wainscoting seemed to frown at

him, follow him with their painted eyes as though watching his movements when he paced the room, and even when he walked in the grounds every tree even seemed to conceal a dark form, and he dreaded lest some one might be there, watching the opportunity to assassinate him.

Sanderson seldom journeyed far.

Occasionally he paid a visit to the "Blue Lobster" or the "Yellow Alligator," and then he dropped in as if by accident, although it was in reality to hear the news discussed by those engaged upon the sea board.

On one of these journeys to Portsmouth he heard something that rather surprised him.

A swift-sailing, clipper-built schooner had just arrived from New Spain; having occasion to call at the Spanish island with letters and dispatches for the governor, the captain, of course, became acquainted with the disaster that had fallen upon the settlement.

The death of Gonsalvo, the destruction of the Spanish fortification, and the almost entire annihilation of the pirate hoarde, drew the attention of all ears, and set every mouth agape.

The bluff seamen who narrated this failed not to interlude his yarn with fitting imprecations and to paint the scene in glowing colours, frequently making use of the expression, "God bless Admiral Tom!" which made Sanderson feel exceedingly unpleasant.

"Who is this Admiral Tom?" he at length ventured to ask, when the man had explained that these glorious achievements had been executed by a combined force of buccaneers and smugglers, under the skilful generalship of a boy buccaneer chief.

"Well," replied the old salt, who in the interval had finished his glass of steaming hot grog, "Admiral Tom is no other individual than Captain Tom Drake—him as they calls the pirate. But, swamp my old shoes, if he aint more of a pirate hunter to my mind. They made him admiral, do you see, when they hoisted the Union Jack above the ruins, just to show as how that the victory was gained by them as was of true British pluck."

A loud cheer for Admiral Tom, and a loud thumping of glasses and jugs upon the tables, greeted this explanation.

"Admiral Tom—Admiral Tom and his English Hearts of Oak!" was thundered throughout the spacious room.

"He'll be hung," said Sanderson, when the uproar for a moment ceased.

"And so will you," roared the tar who had spun the yarn, quite ignorant of whom Sanderson was.

This was a home thrust he did not expect, and it made him quite uncomfortable—indeed, he wished he had never spoken.

Curiosity once aroused, the questions put to the old salt were, of course, very numerous.

His yarning propensities being great, he therefore added a little to the truth on his own account, so that Admiral Tom and his boy buccaneers were looked favourably upon, even by those who were, for obvious reasons, inclined to go against them.

The community being made up of a sprinkling of man-o'-war's-men, marines, and a few smugglers and bum-boatmen, besides the men of the schooner and the chafing Sanderson, their opinions, of course, differed materially.

Old Zack, the worthy host of the "Yellow Alligator," we need scarcely add, did a roaring trade.

Availing themselves of the excuse for indulging in an extra jorum of rum and ale, the orders of the guests to replenish were very numerous.

"Hurrah for Admiral Tom Drake and his boy buccaneers, Old England's true Hearts of Oak!" roared out the blue jackets and marines who had come on shore for a jovial spree from a smart frigate lying in the Sound.

And this being the signal for another bout of applause and boisterous merriment, Sanderson, availing himself of the uproar, slunk out and soon quitted the precincts of the "Yellow Alligator."

CHAPTER CCXLI.

HARRY VERE IS SHOT DOWN FROM HIS GIDDY PERCH—"FIRE! FIRE!"—CAPTAIN ANGEL AND REUBEN HARPY ARE OUTWITTED.

Boom, bang, boom!

Such were the sounds that awakened the echoes in rapid succession, as the big guns of the "Rover" and the sharp speaking pivots placed along her bulwarks belched forth fire and smoke, and sent forth their dread messengers of death.

Captain Angel raved and tore his hair.

His ship was so placed that her shots would have to pass through the hull of the "Spitfire" in order to speed their way in the direction of the "Rover."

With the two ships he was so hampered that he could not decide for the best, whether to cast the "Spitfire" adrift and risk the chance of picking her up again after he had fought the "Rover," or whether to bring all the "Spitfire's" guns to the one side, and thus endeavour to beat off the enemy.

Those of the crew of the "Spitfire" who had not been slain in the fight, or mercilessly butchered for sport, were now battened down in her hold, and therefore his own men had the clear run and free use of both decks.

After mature reflection, and having taken in his position with a skilful eye, Captain Angel decided to try the effect of the "Spitfire's" guns, "For," said he to his lieutenant, Harpy, who was each moment trembling for the masts, the firing may cause a reaction in the air, or the concussion of the guns may cause the vessels to turn round, thus assisting our rudders which are now hanging to their stern posts entirely useless."

"A good thought, Captain Ange'," said Reuben Harpy; "the same thought entered my own mind, and if we have need of more men cannot we press some of our prisoners into our service?"

"Not at all. Are you mad? Order our own men at once to quarters, and let us fight pirate to pirate upon the high seas."

Reuben Harpy cast a glance at the cabin door as he turned away. He had been wondering what had kept the captain so long below, but his craven spirit was not bold enough to ask. Dispelling the thought for the present, however, he bade the drummer beat to quarters, and then the hoarse shout was given—

"Larboard quarters, load your guns!"

As his voice died away, and even as the loaders were busied with rammer and shot, the peculiar whizz of a chain-shot was heard in the air, and a moment later the tall masthead to which Harry Vere was so fiendishly bound came crashing down through spars and ropes on to the deck.

Reuben Harpy's face went greener than usual when this spectacle greeted his sight.

Whether the expression of his features was caused by remorse or gratification it was very hard to determine.

Down, down, headforemost, came poor Harry Vere, the chain connecting the smoking red-hot balls still entwined around the broken spar.

A startled cry emanated from those who were engaged near the spot where the spar with its living load fell; and more than one callous heart that had so recently revelled in carpeting the "Spitfire's" deck with gore revolted in horror at the inhuman sight.

Some, too, who had witnessed the brave boy's prowess when opposed to a treble number of blades, and had seen how his bright cutlass flashed when stronger arms than his were opposed to him, now murmured that one so heroic deserved a more honourable death.

And so thought Harry when he was swaying to and fro at that giddy height, with naught but the sky and the ocean for his eye to dwell upon, until the rover ship came in sight, and, making a target of him, sent their shots hurtling around his helpless form.

But it was quite certain that all the pirates did not share in their comrades' opinion.

It was the red-hot shot they were anxious about the most.

As they fell, smoking and with a hiss, upon the deck, bright flames sprang up, the pitchy seams gave them a welcome, and the tarry ropes and dry woodwork offered themselves as sacrifice to the devouring element.

Had not buckets of water been plentifully supplied and thrown on the hissing flames the "Spitfire" would have been all ablaze, those confined below would have been roasted alive, and both vessels would have been destroyed by the explosion of her magazine.

Willing hands, therefore, went speedily to work, and endeavoured to get the chain-shot free of the spar.

But it was so jambed, and had so eaten into the wood, independent of its still being seething hot, that all their efforts to succeed were futile.

Captain Angel quickly saw this.

He had a threefold incentive to save the ship.

"Stand aside there, you lubbers!" he cried. "Sheer off, every one of you. Give me room."

Then, with a battle-axe he had snatched from the deck, he sprang between the pirates, who drew aside, and with his own hand severed the rope with which he had, only a short time before, ordered Harry to be bound to the mast.

Then the spar, with the still seething iron attached to it, was lifted by the pirates, and with a loud cheer was thrown hissing into the sea.

But where was Harry Vere?

When the pirates looked round he was gone.

Captain Angel, however, did not miss him.

Another red-hot shot set fire to the fore-rigging of the "Spitfire," and the flames running along the fore-yard arm, caught the rigging of the pirate ship.

"Fire—fire!" shrieked Reuben Harpy, whose craven heart fairly quailed under this new disaster. "Fire—fire! Jump aboard, men, at once!"

Captain Angel had already reached his quarter-deck.

Having issued orders that the head sails, which were on fire, should be cut away, and, while the fire party rigged the pumps and draw buckets to drench the spars and rigging with sea water, he shouted to his men to sever the ropes that held the "Spitfire" crunching at his vessel's side.

A breeze having sprung up, and the sails of both vessels being set, the "Spitfire" soon swung clear of her opponent, and placed a cable's length of space between them.

The flames by this time had taken good hold of the sails and rigging of both ships, but those on board of the "Spitfire" were not idle.

Jerry Mizzen and Bob Hauler, from the very moment that they were thrust down below, and the hatches battened down upon them, had devoted themselves to the task of regaining their liberty at all hazards.

Armed with crowbars, and assisted by those of the crew, who were not too disabled, they prized down the planking of the bulkhead and made a passage through the lumber in the hold, so that they soon found themselves beneath the floor of the cabin.

Here they listened, and hearing Harry's voice as he rushed below, on being liberated from the spar, exchanging a few comforting words with Minnie, Bob knocked up, that is struck the under part of the flooring with his crowbar, and Harry, recognising his cheerful hail, cut the lashings of the lazarette hatch and raised it.

To assist each other up through the hole was but the work of a twinkling.

"Now, lads!" Harry said, "waste no time in words; our lives depend upon the promptitude of our actions."

"Aye—aye!" echoed Bob and Jerry.

"Well, then, arm yourselves to the very teeth from the chest there, and prepare with me to defend the cabin from the incursions of these piratical fiends with your lives."

"Aye—aye!" was the general but subdued response given to his words by the small but devoted little band.

Having effectually barricaded the cabin door with sea chests and such furniture as came to hand. They then waited in silence for Captain Angel and his myrmidons to commence the attack.

Harry Vere, Jerry Mizzen, and Micky, the Marine, covered the skylight opening with their pistols and musket, and Minnie, with a brace of small duelling pistols, grasped firmly in her delicate white hands, stood in the background between the stern windows.

All Harry's persuasion that she should seek safety from a stray shot in one of the side cabins was unavailing.

"I will share your risk," she said, bravely, "and die, if need be, with you, noble comrades of my beloved and absent Tom!"

At this juncture, however, Reuben's cry reached their ears and filled their minds with doubt and trepidation.

What could it mean?

The bustle of feet as the pirates hastily rushed to their own ship gave the required answer.

"We are in danger, we shall be roasted alive!" he whispered to his companions. "Let us rush on deck, and defend ourselves like men!"

Then, without another word, the barricade was torn down and hurled aside, and Harry, followed by his gallant few, reached the deck just as the vessels were widening their distance, and the foremast with its yards and sails was enveloped in a pyramid of flame.

CHAPTER CCXLII.

THE SEA EMERALD WORKS ITS POTENT SPELL— ADMIRAL TOM IS BLOWN UP WITH THE DEATH PIRATES' SHIP.

IMPELLED by the action of a favouring breeze, which bellied each sail, and rendered each sheet as taut as a harp string, the "Will-o'-the-Wisp" cleft the foam as she sped on her way to meet the ship that was sailing towards her from an opposite direction.

Every hand, every soul on board Admiral Tom's swift-sailing craft, was in excitement at that moment, for the oncoming ship bore the Death Pirate's unmistakeable flag, and our hero had announced his intention to give him battle.

And this was no idle boast.

As soon as the Death Pirate's ship was in range Iron Arm laid the long bow gun, and with his avenging hand sent a shot flying over the waters.

The effect was electrical.

The iron missile struck the fore part of the Death Pirate's ship, and caused the bowsprit with its long jibboom to snap off close to the stem and fall into the sea.

The Death Pirate raved and foamed with fury as the ship thus became disabled. He clutched his ponderous weapon and seemed as if he could have flown through the intervening space that divided him from Tom's ship.

He would have set his mysterious machinery to work, and have poured a destructive broadside into the "Will-o'-the-Wisp," but for an object he had in view.

His ship, disabled as she was, however, still leaped over the waves, and with a giant stride, as if propelled by some inhuman power, dashed alongside Tom Drake's vessel.

Then, with a deafening and soul-sickening shout, the Death Pirate leapt on to Admiral Tom's deck, and cut his way through the opposing mass, to where the boy chief was already prepared to meet him.

As their eyes met, and the admiral's keen blade turned aside the deadly blow, hurled at him by the Death Pirate's ponderous battle axe, the fore yard arm of the pirate ship snapped off close in the slings, fell with a crash on to the "Will-o'-the-Wisp's" quarter-deck, and felled our hero senseless at his adversary's feet.

A loud mocking laugh then burst from the exultant pirate.

"Mine, mine, you are in my power now, Admiral Tom! But before I scatter your brains to the four winds, I will have my revenge. I will possess the miniature of your peerless bride, the love token she gave you to wear next to your heart."

As he gave a bitter laugh he bent down over the prostrate boy, and, before any of the buccaneers, who were hotly engaged with the pirates, could stay his hand or offer him the least opposition, he tore open the young admiral's corset, and grasped what he thought was the miniature.

"Ha, ha, ha! Let me gaze at the lovely features so that when I meet her I may know I am not mistaken. Ha, ha, ha!"

It was the little bag, however, that he had clutched, and as he tore it open, and his eye rested on the big emerald, his blood coursed through his brain like molten lead.

"Ha, ha, ha! the mystic gem. 'Tis well. Already have I sold my soul to perdition to gain it. Now it is mine!"

He looked horrible. His ghastly mask lit up suddenly with a crimson halo. The potent power of the green diamond had already commenced to work its mischief upon him. He was doomed like the rest.

Doomed, aye! There was no escape for him.

Doctor Shrike, who was looking up the hatchway praying for some victim to operate upon, saw the glittering gem, and incited to fury by its brilliant and dazzling beauty, he sprang like a maniac upon the pirate, and seizing the blazing jewel in one hand, he with the other thrust his long dissecting knife to the tyrant's heart.

As he sank with a groan, another form sprang suddenly to his side. It was the black executioner, and he being too late to save the life of his chief, slashed off the doctor's head with his broad-bladed scimitar, and snatching the jewel from his victim's stiffening hand, ran wildly back to gain his ship.

But too late!

Iron Arm was there at the gangway just in time to bar his progress, and with his heavy mace the giant felled him brainless on the gory deck.

The fierce avenger had also caught a glance of the glittering gem. He knew what it was, and so, with a cry of joy, he stooped to clutch it, but as he did so, Jacop, who had been an unseen witness of all that passed, taking advantage of his recumbent position, dashed out the giant's brains, and, catching up the coveted emerald, darted below out of sight.

Admiral Tom had by this time come to. One swift glance around he took, as he rose erect on his feet, and he saw how critical was his position.

"Dead! dead! dead!" he muttered, as he strode over three well-known forms. "Now will I see whether my darling Minnie is in the cabin of the death tyrant's ship."

He had forgotten the emerald now.

He leapt aboard the pirate barque like a cat, and descended to the cabin without opposition. Then he searched about with no avail, until he caught the sound of voices pleading for help.

The sound came up from beneath him, and so he had to descend to the lower deck by means of a hatchway in the steerage, and as he flew down the ladder, a man dashed past him bearing a flaming torch.

While he stood watching the direction of the light, and wondering if he should follow it, a low hissing sound startled him, then a phiz, phiz, which was quickly followed by a loud and deafening report, and the pirate ship was blown up into the air.

*   *   *   *   *   *

Days have passed—days during which Admiral Tom had laid unconscious hovering between life and death, and now, when he returned, as it were, to life, he still had the bellowing sound of the explosion in his ear.

Naturally no attention had been spared to bring him round.

Zello had watched faithfully and tenderly by his side, and Ben Barnacle, assisted by the busy Jacop, had administered such drugs as were calculated to hasten Tom's recovery.

A brave heart and a strong constitution soon accomplished the rest. In a few days he was strong, and learnt how miraculous he was saved, and also was informed how that two others were picked up from among the charred and floating débris.

"What, Barnacle!" exclaimed Tom, as he reclined on a cushion on the quarter-deck to get the benefit of the sea air, "Mrs. Harpy and my poor misguided Uncle John Gregory are on board the "Will-o'-the-Wisp?"

"As true as fate, admiral, they are in the sick bay, and are not likely to leave it for a while."

"Then I must. Hark, what was that?"

"I heard nothing," said old Ben.

"Not the report of a cannon?"

"No; it must be a fancy on your part, the explosion still ringing in your ears."

"Not so; there it is again," cried Admiral Tom, springing suddenly to his feet. "It sounds away to the eastward. Clap on sail, and point our vessel's head in that direction."

By this time the sound grew so distinct as to be heard by all, and as night drew on apace Admiral Tom and his middy crew were anxious to learn the cause of it.

As time wore on, a bright glare reflected in the fleecy clouds, led them to expect that a ship was on fire, and the crew probably in distress.

The sudden silence of the guns favoured this supposition.

At length, however, the flames themselves were in sight, and then the blazing spars and even the hulls of the blazing ships came into view, whilst the rover, who had ceased firing to cool his loud-mouth cannon, was observable in the distance.

At the masthead of the tallest burning ship Admiral Tom readily descried the grim flag of Captain Angel—the white ground with the black skull and cross-bones could not be mistaken—and so the "Will-o'-the-Wisp" bore down upon her first, as Tom Drake had a long-pending score to settle with her captain.

"Aha! Captain Angel, I come," he thundered, sending his voice over the waves. "Prepare; your doom is near!"

And so it was.

A bright stream of fire ran down the mast, made its way through the deck into the hold, and, catching hold of several barrels of tar, found its way to the fore magazine.

Then followed a terrible hissing, serpent-like sound. The masts tottered, and the yielding decks upheaved; and then, with a loud explosion that strongly agitated the sea, the ship of Captain Angel was sent in shattered fragments hurtling into the air.

CHAPTER CCXLIII.

ADMIRAL TOM BOARDS THE "SPITFIRE"—THE MEETING BETWEEN TOM AND HIS SWEETHEART, MINNIE—ADMIRAL ELLIS AND HIS OFFICERS STRIKE THEIR COLOURS TO RAIS HASSAN—TOM DRAKE TO THE RESCUE—VICTORY—JENNY VERE'S RUSE—HOMEWARD, OH!

WHEN the noise and the shock had subsided, Admiral Tom then turned his attention upon the burning vessel, and his ship's prow advanced towards her. He saw that her crew were in the rigging chopping away the burning sails and yards on the foremast.

Even as he looked the topmast, eaten through by the devouring element, began to sway dangerously to and fro with the vessel's motion, and as it came down with a deafening crash, the young admiral heard a voice which he immediately recognised as Harry's.

To drop a boat and pull to the dismantled "Spitfire" was the next work of him and a few of his chosen hands, and when he boarded the ship he listened eagerly to the brief narrative told by Harry Vere.

"Curse him, he is gone, or I should have torn his very heart out," he cried passionately, referring to Captain Angel. "To pollute my spotless dove with his foul blasphemous tongue would have warranted the dyeing of my sword in his blood."

"But what of Minnie," he added, stamping his foot, "Where is she now, Harry Vere?"

"Here," cried a low quivering voice, "here, darling Tom," and at the same instant Minnie was on deck and nestled to his breast like a trembling bird.

Let us pass over the meeting.

The "Spitfire" now was in dire calamity.

The mainmast was on fire, the decks and the foremast of the ship in one mass of fork-tongued flames, so that it was necessary to desert her, and seek safety on board the "Will-o'-the-Wisp."

Admiral Tom was ripe for vengeance then.

He steered after the rover barque that had thus unwittingly almost deprived him of his love, and a swift and flying chase was kept up for several days.

Then a mist suddenly rose and hid the chase from view, and when some hours later it cleared away Admiral Tom, from his quarter-deck, descried two Algerian galleys towing a dismantled man-of-war.

"A Frenchman, by Jove," said Harry Vere, who stood in his place beside his youthful commander. "She's struck, and no British wall of oak could ever do that."

But he was mistaken.

The man-of-war was an English frigate, once taut and trim, and commanded by the perturbable Admiral Ellis, who, misguided by his first lieutenant, Gaston, and his next in command, Lord Kilcrew, had fallen into the hands of the redoubtable Corsair, Rais Hassan, and one of the pirate galleys of the fleet.

The figurehead was all Tom recognised the frigate by, and this he did with the aid of a private list, which gave him the rank, build, armament, and general description of every vessel in King George's service.

To pass the word to prepare for action was therefore his first determination—although he felt loth to risk the lives of so many helpless ones as he then had on board the "Will-o'-the-Wisp."

But to be brief, the battle was victorious.

Although the action was splendidly entered into on both sides, Tom's splendid judgment weighed heavily against the superiority of metal.

In less than an hour Tom had put the galley to flight, boarded Rais Hassan's ship, and retaken the frigate with barely the loss of a man.

Rais Hassan was in a towering rage.

For when he should towe his capture into port it would be time for him to wed his English bride, and the thought was agony so intense that he cursed the very beard he had shorn of its patriarchal dignity to enslave her.

When Mrs. Drake and Jenny Vere heard by the shouts that an English crew were assailing the Corsairs, their hearts, which had been the toys of shattered hopes and endless fears, began to sway tremblingly in the balance.

When Jenny heard that Admiral Tom was the name of the victor, and that he was on board the galley, she crept on deck to ascertain whether it was the long looked-for Captain Drake.

When Hassan saw her, he, with vengeful hies, flew towards her and pressed her back, when the gallant Tom, moved to pity by her exquisite form and loveliness, smote him to the deck.

As yet neither Tom nor Jenny had recognised each other, and she, now dressed as a Corsair maiden, was enabled to steal a side, long glance at his altered face without Tom discovering her own.

But it was his voice she mainly depended upon, and so she effected a ruse in kneeling down by the side of the wounded Corsair, and raising his head, so as to cause the victorious admiral to speak.

And the ruse proved successful. Joy beamed in her heart, and a scene such as would baffle every pen to describe hereafter ensued.

To drive every pirate overboard into the sea, excepting the Rais, who was made hostage for the safety of Admiral Ellis and his officers, who were borne away to captivity on board the fugitive galley, was to Tom's middies capital sport.

And so, with the frigate and the Corsair galley in tow, the "Will-o'-the-Wisp" stood for the shores of old England, determined to show King George that Admiral Tom Drake, and his buccaneer crew, were not cringing rebels, as they were proscribed, but true English Hearts of Oak.

* * * * * *

"Homeward, oh!" What a joyful sound, especially to those who have been so long absent, and who have gone through such perils as we have narrated.

What memories, too—visions of home—the welcome words awakened, for the young middies on Admiral Tom's ship were but mortal, and, therefore, their minds reverted to their homes, their parents, sweethearts, friends, and above all the welcome, kind or otherwise, they were likely to receive.

Bob Hauler and Jerry Mizzen shared in these hopes and fears, but they produced little or no effect on their naturally jovial dispositions.

Their minds continually reverted to the time when they sat in the hollow in the side of the cliff, and saw our young hero tumbled down from aloft into the sea by his dastardly cousin, Reuben Hurpy.

"Aye, aye, Bob!" Jerry remarked, as he drew an uncorked bottle from the bosom of his shirt. "We gloried in the delightful stuff in them days, and why shouldn't we now? Here's a health to all our friends, and as hard biscuit and toothless jaws to them as is our enemies!"

Bob took a good pull at the rum bottle, during which time Jerry indulged in a few moments' thought.

"I should like to see them days over again, Jerry," he said at length. "Who'd a' thought we'd ever live to see that young whelp, as we called him, when he dropped like a plummet into the ocean and disturbed our quiet moments, a admiral?"

"Not me, Bob, old messmate. I wonder what the Admiralty will have to say to us if we run into Portsmouth in this trim? Do you think they'll try us as pirates, and ——"

"Run us up to the yardarm," interposed Bob Hauler. "That's most likely. And if you take my advice you'll lay in a good lining of grog before we go on the journey, for it's only a short trip to the jewel-block, but its a long journey for the likes of us from here to heaven."

"And no ports half-way," suggested Jerry; "so let's empty this marine, and throw his body overboard."

"Werry good—werry good indeed! That's capital advice," said a muffled voice, which seemed to proceed from a dark corner of the forecastle. "A dead marine's no use at all, but a live 'un should be always respected. If you've a toothful of that 'ere throat-oil left I'd like to grease my throttle with it."

"Come out of that, then," said Jerry Mizzen; "what are you skulking about and listening to our conflab for? Who are you, you lubberly swab? Take that, and share it among you."

Having drained the bottle to its last dregs, Jerry, as he spoke, hurled the bottle with great force into the corner, which act did not only elicit a dismal howl, but brought forth a doleful-looking object from that quarter.

"Hallo, Mickey, it's you, is it?" said Bob, as he caught sight of the marine's abject and deplorable-looking visage. "Why, you're doubled up like a rope yarn, old chum. What's taken the ram-rod out of your backbone, and the starch out of your anatomy? Has Jacob been giving you a dose of squills?"

"Bilge-water, you mean," replied Mickey, dolefully. "The warmint gave me a dose of comfort as he called it, but I'll be even with him. He wants to poison me, I'm sure, because I know— I know—well—something."

"You do, eh?" said Bob Hauler, in a dubious tone; "you've been watching him the same as you have us, I 'spose? Well, look out, my noble eavesdropper, or I may drop down on you with a drop of comfort that will settle you."

The marine looked at Bob with an expression of amazement.

"What do you mean?" he asked.

"Just what I say. If you're going to turn sneak, why, we'll bottle you up and cork you, that's all; so clear out, for we're ill friends arter this."

"I hope not," said Mickey, in a trembling voice. "I don't want to fall out with either of you, but I've learnt something, and if you hadn't a' thrown that confounded bottle at me, and doubled me up, I'd a' told you something to your advantage."

"You would?" exclaimed Jerry.

"Yes; but you'll know it all in time, perhaps when it's too late; but I'm too dry to hold a long palaver, so I'll pay a visit to the water cask."

"And take jolly good care you don't fall through the bung-hole," sneered Bob, "for no one 'll pull you out—d'ye mind me?—but some-one may give you a topper on the head with a hand-spike."

As Bob spoke he pulled the sleeve of Jerry Mizzen, and, giving the discomfited marine a vicious look, Hauler led his companion on deck.

"We must watch him," said Bob, as he and Jerry took up their accustomed post between the knight heads. "I never did like a jolly, and we were fools to trust him with our secrets, or even to allow him to share our company."

"You're right, Bob, we don't do it again; but he ain't found out the secret entrance to the smugglers' cave. We may have spoken to him about our old haunts, but we never told him how to visit 'em."

"Of course not. Who knows but that we may have to return to them again? I for one would rather risk bullet and steel in the contraband service than go a flying journey aloft on the tail end of a rope, Jerry."

In the meantime the "Will-o'-the-Wisp," with every inch of canvas she could spread wooing the breeze, sped gaily towards that formidable and towering fortress, Gibraltar

With the dead weight towing astern, of course her progress was somewhat impeded, although jury masts had been rigged on board the dismantled vessels, and square sails spread to ease the strain on the stout hawser by which the frigate and corsair galley were towed.

Admiral Tom seldom left the deck.

His anxiety for the safety of his prizes was so great that sleep seemed to have totally forsaken him.

He took every precaution to prevent his being surprised and having his captures taken from him by the Corsair fleet, his guns on both sides being loaded and run out, and their crews sleeping at their quarters, ready for action at the young commander's word.

At each masthead, too, a watch was stationed, and not an object, even to the floating turtle basking in the sun, escaped the keen scrutiny of Admiral Tom's quick eye and powerful glass.

But, whilst danger was so strictly guarded off on deck, it was treated below with a sort of negligence.

Tom, in fact, never dreamed of its lurking in that quarter.

It had never occurred to him that Zelie, the beautiful, loving, and impulsive Arabian girl, would regard her mistress, Minnie Atherton, with a jealous eye.

He had never thought that her proud spirit would rebel against the lowering of her dignity —for such it was—for previous to Minnie coming on board Zelie had none to share with her the love she entertained towards our hero, or stand between herself and the boy chief, whom she idolised.

Doubtless the young admiral's mind was too engrossed with other matters to even suspect such a possibility, and, therefore, Zelie had more opportunity of encouraging the green-eyed and deadly monster that daily and hourly grew and entwined itself more firmly around her susceptible heart.

But this feeling the jealous maiden carefully guarded from the females, who now almost entirely occupied the cabin and its state-room.

Neither by word or gesture did she betray the least symptoms that she was unhappy.

Ever cheerful in their presence, she indeed affected to do their bidding with a willingness that won both their gratitude and praise, and gained for her their confidence, so much so that Mrs. Drake even unbosomed to her many of her cherished secrets.

But Zelie cared not for these favours.

Her whole thoughts were centered in one object.

She desired to bring upon Minnie Atherton the disfavour of the crew, and by this means to render her less significant in the eyes of Admiral Tom.

But how could she accomplish this alone?

How compass the disfavour of one who was so dearly beloved and almost worshipped by the crew?

She must find an accessory; but whom could she trust?

To whom could she venture to divulge the deadly secret that like a canker-worm was devouring her heart?

Discovery, she knew, would bring upon her banishment—perhaps even death!

What could she do then? The very thought of her helplessness drove her almost to distraction.

As she lay tossing and restless on her sleepless pillow a thought suddenly occurred to her.

In a strong room, which was at times used as a spare powder magazine, in the 'tween decks of the "Will-o'-the-Wisp," a prisoner was confined, and that was no other than Rais Hassan.

He, of course, hated Admiral Tom as deeply as she adored him; and, in fact, it might naturally be surmised that he cherished a deadly hatred towards all on board, Zelie not excepted.

But for all that there was one ray of hope in her favour.

Was she not a native of a clime closely connected with his own, and could she not converse with him in a language known only to a few on board beside themselves?

"Yes," she muttered, as she rose hastily from the couch, and viewed herself in the mirror hung against the wainscot of the cabin, "I will try my subtle power upon him. I will—I will. What——"

Then she relapsed into a state of mental abstraction.

How could he, a prisoner, assist her? He was powerless to aid himself, and he would have willingly paid a heavy ransom for his freedom.

"Ah! I have it," she muttered, suddenly, as the hot blood tinged her olive cheek and caused it to tingle; "I will promise him his liberty if he will only follow my instructions. He must fire the ship, and I must provide him with the means of doing so; but none, saving ourselves, shall know I have visited his prison."

She looked like a demon now. With her dark dishevelled hair and her large black eyes dilating wildly, she stood for a few seconds regarding herself in the mirror, and then she was decided.

"I must disguise myself," she said; "and in this drawer I have the means to do so. Ah! Minnie Atherton, I am going to impersonate you, but not for the love I bear you—no, no! but to accomplish my design I am compelled to do that at which my very soul revolts—robe myself in the attire that has encircled your hated form."

So saying, she took from the drawer a dress similar to that which was worn by Minnie on the previous day; and, with pomatum and a yellowish powder, she hid the colour of her hair, and soon had her disguise completed.

"There," she said, in a tone which expressed satisfaction, as she gave a finishing touch to her enamelled cheeks; "none can recognise me now. I am safe, for who besides my loved Admiral Tom dare to gaze too closely into the eyes and features of, as they will take mine to be, his adored affianced bride. None," she muttered, softly, as she cautiously opened the door of her state-room and listened. "All is clear," she added, "all is stillness save for the grinding of those big ropes, the noise of the steering wheel, and the creaking of these bulkheads."

There was a footstep on deck, however, pacing up and down.

That she knew was Admiral Tom's.

Other footsteps, too, walked aft, and those, by their heavy tread, she recognised as Ben Barnacle's.

Thus there were two on deck that she wished to avoid, and now her task was to find out who kept sentry over the hatchway leading to the Corsair captain's cell.

This was a bold and dangerous step; but, so fident of the success of her disguise, she did not flinch from it; in fact, she reached the spot sooner than she was aware, and found the sentry on his post asleep.

To glide softly past him, and approach the iron bars that had been fitted in the door of the ship's prison for the admittance of air and the dim light cast by the smoky lamp suspended from a beam just over where the unconscious sentry slept, took Zelie but an instant.

Startled by her sudden appearance, the Corsair chief rose from his recumbent posture, and gazed at her in wonderment.

"Silence! — hush!" she whispered, in his native tongue.

And, thus admonished, Rais Hassan listened in silent wonderment to all she said, at the close of which conference she departed with an assurance that the captive Corsair would do all she might require of him.

And that was not much, materially speaking.

She having provided him with some oakum-tarred rope—and the means of ignition, Rais Hassan was to set light to it in his cell, and when the smoke was discovered, and the necessary confusion ensued, Zelie was to effect his release.

This all seemed palpable enough, especially to the Corsair, who, like a drowning man, grasped at anything, never for an instant hesitating to reflect whether it could really murder him any assistance or not.

Unwilling to unnecessarily protract her stay, Zelie then prepared to pass the sentry; but in his sleep he had moved and so lay as to block her passage up the ladder, thus causing her to seek an exit from the lower deck by another hatchway.

This brought her in close contact with the sick bay in which Jacop and one or two wounded seamen slept, and, being curious to learn whether Jacop was there, the emboldened girl drew the canvas curtain that closed the entrance aside and peered in.

And the sight she saw astonished her.

Jacop was fast asleep, but in his hand was firmly clasped the little bag which Zelie felt certain she had once seen in possession of Admiral Tom.

It was only a cursory glance she obtained of it on that occasion, as our hero was at the time hiding it away, but for all that, and although she could only see part of it now, she was fully assured it was the same.

But how came Jacop in possession of it?

How did the late vampire's assistant remove it from its fastening round the neck of Admiral Tom?

This was a mystery she was determined to solve there and then.

One glance at the hammocks around satisfied her that their occupants were asleep.

To creep softly to the side of Jacop was, therefore, her first act, and then to take hold of his hand and endeavour, by a gentle pressure, to remove his fingers from his coveted treasure was the next.

But in this she signally failed.

Jacop, although lying on his back, and snoring loud enough to deaden the noise made by the two stout tow-ropes grinding upon the taffrail, and to all appearance buried in as profound a slumber as that indulged in by the Seven Sleepers, woke up with a start, and gazed at the apparition before him in utter bewilderment.

Deceived by the effectual disguise, he of

course readily surmised that Zelie was no other person, either in shadow or substance, than Minnie Atherton.

But what brought her there?

To what strange and, to him, inexplicable cause was he indebted to her for this visit?

"Y-yes. Wh-wh-what do you want, lady?" he stammered out as soon as he could command his power of speech. "Are you a gh-gh-ghost?"

Such a suggestion was not lost upon the quick-witted girl.

"I'm a spectre," she said, in a hollow whisper. "I am Minnie Atherton in shadow but not in substance, and I have come here to discover a theft."

Jacop was more terrified than ever.

He broke out all over in a profuse sweat.

His guilty conscience, of course, accused him of the theft of the big sea emerald; but, then, how could anyone but himself know of it, as the one from whose hand he had taken it was dead?

This puzzled him, and, above all, aroused him to a more perfect state of consciousness.

In his terror he had glided the hand with his treasure in it beneath the blanket, and, with the knowledge that it was safe, he was better able to reflect.

As he did so, and gazed with dilated eyes at the face of his nocturnal visitor, he detected something peculiar about that part of the face which was exposed, and now the experience taught him by the practise of his profession stood him in good stead.

It was a small patch of dark skin, the natural colour of Zelie's before she covered it with the enamel, and, as his practised eye noted the difference between the parts where the enamel still adhered and the part where it was removed, Jacop at once detected the imposition.

The voice, too, he remembered was not so soft and musical as Minnie's, and the very enamel was some he had prepared, acting under the instructions of his late master, Doctor Shrike.

Zelie could not but notice how Jacop's fears gradually melted away.

It alarmed her.

Having lost confidence, she felt that her own power of deceit was rapidly weakening.

As a last resource, nevertheless, she thought she would again try her voice on the boy, and endeavour to inspire him with terror.

"And so, mortal," she said, in the same hollow tone as before, "your callous heart refuses even to relent, therefore you are doomed—doomed to everlasting torment—that is, if you escape the punishment which your crime deserves."

Jacop, although he was too much used to handling the ghastly relics of the dead to be afraid of anything earthly, was slightly inclined to believe in ghosts, and the deathly pallor was stealing over his features again when Zelie, impelled by a sudden violent motion of the ship, bumped against his hammock.

This was a clear proof of substance instead of shadow.

"You are not a ghost—you are alive," he muttered, his parched tongue cleaving to the roof of his mouth.

"All the worse for you," was Zelie's angry and impulsive reply. "You know me, I see, and therefore I must bind you to silence on the subject."

"What for? I can't understand why you have come here," said Jacop, opening his eyes in surprise and looking doubtful.

"Nor I," muttered Zelie to herself. "But now I am here I must not sacrifice my chance of revenge without a struggle. Do you know," she added, addressing Jacop, "that that packet you have I have seen in the hands of our admiral, and that if it was traced to your possession it would be means of the signing of your death warrant."

Jacop shuddered.

He liked not the idea of being put to death, especially as the "Will-o'-the-Wisp" was bound to Old England, and he had conjured up visions of enjoyment on shore.

As yet he had not the remotest idea of the immense value of the green sea emerald. That it was costly, and would fetch him a good sum he well knew, and that it was worth keeping, even if he had to commit some crime to enable him to do so, there was not a doubt.

"But you will not betray me," he said, his teeth meanwhile chattering like a pair of castanets. "You dare not, or—"

"I dare do anything," replied the crafty maiden, "to obtain revenge—sweet, sweet, revenge! I would sacrifice a thousand lives, and my own afterwards if need be."

Jacop, who had rolled into his hammock in his clothes, so as to enable him to bestow immediate attention on his patients, if needed, now slid out on to the floor.

"A thousand lives!" he gasped, as a choking sensation rose in his throat. "Then what would my miserable life be compared with so many?"

"Naught," Zelie hissed, spitefully; "but I do not want to take your wretched life. I have not even made up my mind to seek the life of others. Did I so wish you know I am armed with the power. Did you not provide me with a subtle poison?"

"I did," replied Jacop, with a shudder.

He was not clear as to what Zelie was aiming at.

Was her speech meant to convey the hint that she could poison him if she so chose, or anyone else who attempted to thwart her, or what?

"Well, then," said Zelie, who seemed at once to divine his thoughts, "having reminded you of the power I hold, you will see I need no one's assistance in that way; but you can aid me, nevertheless. You can render me a service I shall never forget, for which, no matter what I do for you, I shall feel that you are never repaid. "What say you?"

As she spoke she glanced into his eyes, and, placing her hand upon his shoulder, awaited his reply.

Her basilisk-like glance had its fascinating effect upon him.

The warmth from her hand also worked its electricity upon him, and made him feel he had not the power of resistance.

"What think you about it?" she said, alluding to the subject again. "Jacop, I await your answer."

"Speak, speak then, and tell me what you would have me do. I feel that I cannot deny you any request; but be merciful, I pray, for I have not the courage to commit a cold-blooded murder."

BEN BARNACLE AND HARRY VERE ON BOARD THE FLAG SHIP.

When the word "Murder!" was uttered by Jacop's white and bloodless lips his eyes fixed themselves on the glittering orbs of his remorseless but beautiful temptress with a glassy stare.

His eyeballs appeared to protrude from their sockets, and seemed as if ready to start from his head.

Murder! and in cold blood, too.

The thought was more than the craven-hearted Jacop could withstand.

It sent an icy chill through his frame, and almost caused the pulsation of his heart to cease.

Zelie read his thoughts in a moment.

Although she was not averse to making the cringing Jacop the tool of her abominations, she in her inmost heart loathed him.

Even now, with her mind overflowing with jealous hatred, and her brain awhirl with evil passions, the beautiful demon could not help calling to mind the time when Dr. Shrike, aided by his now craven-hearted assistant, carved the heart out from the fair breast of the brave young middy who had fallen in the engagement with the piratical fleet.

Our readers will remember how warmly Zelie rebuked the callous-hearted vampire on that occasion, how she wept for the noble boy when he was laid in a sailor's grave, and how the sorrowing middies indignantly resented the cruel insult to the shot-torn remains of their gallant messmate.

And Zelie, as we have said, thought of this.

"Bah!" exclaimed the corsair maiden, shrinking from him, and eyeing him with ineffable scorn, "you who could assist in dissecting a living man to talk in that cowardly way! But I have no murder on hand for you to perform; I want you to raise a report."

"Ah! a lie," exclaimed Jacop, his eye suddenly brightening.

"Not quite so bad as that even, unless you are closely questioned; but the penalty of your bungling will, I assure you, be certain death."

Jacop went pale again.

77

No matter which way he leaned towards the wishes of this mysterious maiden, he was menaced with death, and she failed not to put it before him in its worst terrors.

How he would be tried and sentenced by the young buccaneer chief—strung up to the yard-arm, to there hang till he was dead, and then afterwards to be cut down and made food of for some hungry shark.

Zelie played her part with the cleverness of a well-trained actress.

There was nothing that Jacop held so much in abhorrence as a shark, and to have a limb taken off by the saw-like teeth of one of those marauders of the deep had ever been considered by him as one of the most cruel and ghastly operations that could be performed.

Whether alive or dead, it mattered not to Jacop, he cared not to be the subject operated upon, and, therefore, the very allusion to one of the carnivorous species was sufficient to make him collapse, like an empty balloon.

Falling upon his knees, he with clasped hands besought his persecutor to spare him.

But Zelie was inexorable.

His choking sobs and almost inaudible voice were music to her ear, and in less time than we record it she had bent him to her will.

When she turned to leave him she had not only his promise to do her bidding, but she had made him breathe a vow that he would never divulge her secret, whether the plot failed or was successful.

As with rapid steps she glided back towards her cabin, and whilst her brain was throbbing with tumultuous joy, a hoarse, muffled voice arrested her progress and caused her to start.

"Who comes? Speak, or I'll fire!"

"Your queen, Minnie Atherton," was Zelie's hasty reply, as she continued to proceed towards her cabin.

But the stern voice arrested her as before with—

"Halt! you have some meaning for this deceit. This disguise, Zelie?"

The Arabian girl shook violently for a moment. Who was this that barred her way, and could address her by name?

She put the question, and the answer being returned in the natural voice of the speaker, she instantly recognised it.

It was that of Mickey the marine, the sentry she had seen asleep at the foot of the ladder below. He had been awakened by the rustle of her dress, and now he confronted her, possessing a knowledge that, however small, must be dangerous to the corsair maiden.

This she knew—the bold manner in which he pronounced her name assured her so, and that guided her in her present course of procedure.

"And, so like a stealthy worm," she said, in a tone mixed up with bitter irony, "you have dogged my footsteps, and have seen and heard——"

"Nay, not like a worm," exclaimed the marine, interrupting her." I have but performed my duty. What I have seen and heard is at present locked up in my own breast; it is in your power to seal it there or to bid me disclose it."

Zelie shrank back instinctively from him.

"Do you use this speech," she said, "to intimidate me?" If so, let me inform you that it is also in my power to denounce you as unworthy of your post. You have slept—I saw you—and to sleep on such duty as is assigned to you, is punishable with death. You will be court-

martialed, found guilty, and then you will be sentenced to die, either by hanging at the yard-arm, walking the plank, or by the leaden bullets of a firing party."

Mickey needed no reminder of this.

"But what proof have you?" said he, determined to put a bold face on the matter and face it out.

"Enough to warrant your execution," Zelie replied, tersely; and then, softening her tone, she added, "I have no desire to compass your death. You can aid me, if you will, and my favour, which I have reserved for princes, shall be your reward."

Mickey's eye suddenly lighted up as she gave him this promise.

A kind word, an encouraging glance from her would have brought him to her feet a cringing slave, ready to do her bidding and to aid her to his utmost in any project she might be contemplating.

Zelie had long noted this fact by his manner and the various pretexts he had made use of to throw himself in her way.

Therefore he was easily thrown off his guard by her set speech, and he replied—

"It is yours to command and mine to obey, fair maiden. Speak—be not afraid. Tell me in plain words what you would have me to do."

And Zelie complied.

But it was not the truth that she told him. She put it to him in this way: that, as she was anxious to frighten Rais Hassan and punish him for the cruel insults he had heaped upon Mrs. Drake and Jenny Vere, she wanted an interview with the prisoner so that she could execute her plan.

"There is no harm in that," said the crafty marine, who at the same time doubted not that there was something more in her mind than she had unburthened to him, but as she drew near to him and presented him with a small star set in brilliants, which she took from around her neck, he was determined to be satisfied with her explanation.

"There," she said, having placed the jewel safely in his grasp, " let this gem be an earnest of my eternal friendship. If you are in peril it will act as a talisman to you, and, should you at any time need my aid, fear not to seek me, and I will render you assistance."

Mickey was quite overpowered.

Clasping her right hand, he raised it to his lips and imprinted a fervent kiss upon it, after which he gave her a list of the sentries who were told off to keep guard over the prisoner, and advised her as to the best time when she could pay her visit to the cell with the least fear of detection.

"It is well," she said. "Now adieu! I feel assured that with you my secret is safe. And I will make it doubly so," she muttered to herself as she glided away. "A bought confederate is seldom to be trusted, and the casket that holds a secret should not have too many openings for its egress."

What she meant will hereafter be disclosed.

CHAPTER CCXLIV.

THE GIBBET—TREACHERY—THE FATAL EMERALD—WON, WOOED, AND WEDDED.

WHEN Sanderson left the "Yellow Alligator," disgusted with its occupants, and chafing with the news he had heard concerning the daring exploits of Admiral Tom, he hastened with all speed to the nearest post-house.

Arrived there he had barely time to fortify

himself with a stiff tumbler of hot brandy, and light a cigar when the coach was ready for starting.

"Aha! just in time, thanks to fortune," said Sanderson, as he drew his hat well down to his ears and, wrapping a thick muffler about his throat, prepared to mount by the side of the driver.

"We shall have it fine and a pleasant journey, I hope," said another passenger who followed Sanderson up and shared with him the seat, "I dislike travelling in bad weather, whether it be wind, snow, hail or rain—in fact, sir, I don't like travelling at all if I can help it, do you?"

But Sanderson was not in a talking humour; his mind was too much occupied with the doings of Admiral Tom Drake, who might at any moment turn up and wreak a terrible vengance upon him for his evil doings and the base means by which he gained possession of the Atherton Estate.

And now, as the coach started on its return journey, Sanderson felt not the buoyancy of one returning home—far from it, he experienced a feeling of dread, and actually envied the ragged, bare-footed little urchins that ran out of the low-roofed cottages to witness the coach go by.

The talkative gentleman was not, however, to be put off with Sanderson's silence, nor would he cease speaking when Sanderson, in an ill-humour, declared that he preferred smoking in silence to talking.

"Ah! well, that is some people's way, sir," he said; "but give me a good, honest, open conversation upon a country road, I say. I suppose, sir, you have heard of that extraordinary, reckless, devil-may-care sort of a fellow, Admiral Tom Drake? Now, what do you think of him?"

"I don't bother my head about such people," was Sanderson's tart reply. "I'd have him hung, drawn, and quartered, as I would all such piratical and dangerous scoundrels who run away with his Majesty's ships!"

"But, sir, report says that King George is in ecstacies over the news; for you see, sir, Spain has made several glaring attempts to lord it over us, and that Spanish island, which is only a few leagues, sir, from the Spanish main, and—and—there are drops in the wind. Rain is coming, sir. Ah! by Jove the man's asleep."

And Sanderson was, too, to all outward appearance. Inwardly, however, he was devouring every word, and cursing his fellow-passenger for dinning the name of Admiral Tom in his much-offended ears.

The sky was now very lowering.

Cold gusts of wind swept across the fields, and caused the passengers to sink out of sight almost into their overcoats.

The rain began to fall and beat in their faces, added to which, and to complete the dreariness of the scene, darkness was drawing on.

The journey was now pursued in silence.

The talkative man, following the example set by his fellow-travellers, muffled himself right up to his eyes, thus impeding his conversational powers.

Hour after hour passed, the post-horses were changed, but the weather continued the same, and Sanderson, who had availed himself of steaming hot potions whenever the opportunity occurred, looked like one in a dream.

And he did dream, too. The forms of old John Gregory and Mrs. Harpy rose up before him, their faces deathly-looking and ghastly;

whilst, with their long arms outstretched towards him, they seemed to accuse him of murdering them.

So much like reality was this that Sanderson was almost tempted to cry out, when a peculiar sound caused him to start and look ahead.

The rain had abated a bit; through a rift in the clouds, the moon, hitherto hidden, now shone forth, and as the coach drew near the plot of ground that marked the cross roads he beheld the ghastly gibbet with its chains swinging to and fro in the night wind, making a clanging sound that sent an unpleasant thrill through the ears of all who heard it.

Sanderson sat like one bereft of reason, staring at the dark, unsightly thing, until he felt as if he would sink through the cushioned seat, when suddenly a dark cloud obscured the moon, leaving each object enshrouded in sable darkness.

With his eyes still riveted in that direction, Sanderson, when the moon again shone forth, uttered a startling cry, for there beneath the outstretched arm of the gallows tree he beheld an object that made all who saw it repeat his awful cry.

The figure was that of an old and wrinkled hag, who supported her bent body with a crook, whilst with her disengaged hand she pointed to heaven and at the terror-distorted features of Sanderson, who fancied that the arm grew in length until the fingers touched his cold, clammy face.

The horses, terrified by the fearful vision, sped rapidly on until the grim gibbet was left far behind and gradually grew smaller in the distance.

Awed by the weird apparition, the passengers maintained a solemn silence, which was only broken by the occasional winding of the guard's horn, until the post-house at which Sanderson had to alight was reached.

On arriving home he found Doctor Birchenhall awaiting him. He had brought news of Admiral Tom, and almost the first words he greeted Sanderson with were those of our hero's name.

"And so you, like the rest, have come to taunt me and din my ears with that hated name; you, who at least should know that, to a gentleman of my wealth and position, the name of such a worthless scoundrel is poison to my ears."

The doctor coloured slightly, and gave a dry cough.

It galled him considerably to hear the nephew of his old friend Gregory spoken of thus, and just when society at large were on the tip-toe of speculation as to whether his Britannic Majesty King George would grant the young admiral a free pardon and allow him to return to his native land, or still pursue him to his death.

News travelled slowly in those primitive days, The account of Admiral Tom's daring exploit n the Mediterranean had not yet reached home.

But enough of this matter has been said.

Doctor Birchinhall saw in the wild, glaring eye of the man before him enough to convince him that Sanderson was going mad, and he left with the full conviction that he would one day become an inmate of his lunatic asylum.

Could he have seen Sanderson an hour or so later on, it would have rewarded him for the trouble he took in having a room prepared for him.

Had he seen him pacing the room with maddened strides, tearing his grizzly locks, and fighting with the air, in which he saw the shadowy forms of his victims pointing at him and pronouncing his doom, the doctor would have beheld in him a raving maniac.

The next day, however, saw Sanderson removed. He had made an attempt upon his wretched life, and had to be confined in a padded room, where he was under the vigilance of a couple of strong and able-bodied keepers.

*   *   *   *   *   *

"Fire—fire—fire!"

"Fire in the lower hold! Fire!"

Such were the cries which rang through the "Will-o'-the-Wisp," and fell with startling vividness upon the ears of those who were seated in their state cabins, reading or otherwise engaged, on the evening succeeding that on which Zelie had held her interview with Jacop.

"Fire—fire!" and the ship's bell accompanied the shouts, as hasty feet responded to the call, showing that the watch below had readily turned out and made for the stations allotted to them in the event of so direful a calamity.

Admiral Tom, although wearied with his long and anxious watch, placed himself at once at the head of his calm but resolute crew.

By his cool and stoical demeanour he quelled the excitement that at first seemed imminent, and sent word by Harry Vere to the ladies to remain quiet and not be alarmed, as the great and terrible danger could not be averted or got over by their wild and frantic outcries.

It was to Mrs. Drake and Mrs. Harpy that this message was chiefly addressed.

And also to John Gregory, who, old, feeble, and unnerved by his terrible sufferings, was at times seized with the weakness of a child.

To Minnie Atherton and Jennie Vere no such caution was needed, and as to Zelie, the corsair maiden, although she shammed much fear, the reader knows she was free from any undue trepidation.

It was her wicked and designing mind that caused it all.

She had prevailed upon the captive to fire the ship, and, having provided him with the means, she neglected the promise she never intended to fulfil, and left him to his fate.

What cared she whether he was roasted or not?

What to her would it be if the ship caught fire and was destroyed?

But the victim of this beautiful demon's plot and passion was yet to feel the force of her iniquity.

When the fire was discovered to be in the lower hold, Jacop, true to his vow, spread the report that he saw a female pass up the hatchway a short time previous to the outbreak, and that, although he could not see her face, he could swear by her dress that it was Minnie.

He was crafty enough to entertain the wounded midshipman and sailors in the sick bay with this as a profound secret, which, of course, was the very way in which to spread the report with lightning swiftness.

Like wildfire it flew from deck to deck, and Jacop soon after was brought before the admiral to repeat his statement.

Admiral Tom was, of course, astounded.

In Jacop's frightened face he failed to detect the foul aspersion, and therefore he resolved, when the alarm was over, to institute amongst the crew the most searching investigation.

By this time Ben Barnacle and a few of his trustiest midshipmen had reached the lower deck, where the first object they stumbled across was the prostrate form of a marine. By his side they also found an empty bottle.

"Why, it's Mickey!" exclaimed one of the mids, as he raised the sentry's head; "and he stinks of rum, too, and that pretty strongly."

"He's been drugged," Ben Barnacle said, as he hastily snatched up the bottle and placed it to his nostrils. "There's as much opium in that bottle now as would serve a Chinese mandarin for a month!"

"Carry him on deck," he added to a couple of the buccaneers, "he'll be as smoke-dried as a side of bacon if he remains here."

The smoke was now so dense and suffocating that old Ben and his followers had to tear off their neckerchiefs and tie them across their mouths before venturing any further.

This done, they groped about in the smoke and darkness until one of them, discovering a red ball of fire through the gloom, raised an outcry.

Turning in its direction, they therefore groped their way to the grated door of the spare magazine, through the bars of which they beheld the cause of the smoke, and at once commenced to batter down the door.

This took but a few seconds, yet it seemed an age, for the dense vapour emitted by the smouldering oakum was so pungent that it set them all sneezing and coughing in a manner that threatened them with being choked.

The fire once found there was no lack of water at hand to quench it. Fire buckets were passed freely up and down the hatchways, and in a few moments nothing remained of the dangerous element but steam and smoke.

In the midst of this the half-dead form of the Corsair captain was dragged from his prison-house and carried into fresh air, when slight hopes of his recovery were entertained.

Meanwhile a scene no less exciting, but of a totally different character, was being enacted on the middle or main deck.

The wounded seamen in the sick bay, having listened to Jacob's artfully-concocted story, excited by its recital and the stifling vapour that now poured up the hatchways and insinuated itself into every hole and corner of the ship, leaped from their hammocks and vowed vengeance on the young girl whom they hastily concluded had consigned them to a terrible and agonising death.

One, a young middy, whose shot-torn hand was slung in a handkerchief about his neck, called aloud for vengeance.

"Lads," he said, "let us arm and seek this female fiend, and cut out her heart, which surely must be as black as Hades."

"Aye—aye!" was the response of his shipmates. "To the after cabin. Away!"

And so, without a moment's reflection, they followed the madcap young middy to the cabin door, which they burst open with a crash, and beheld two females, clasped in each other's arms, standing near one of the cabin windows bathed in tears.

The ladies, startled by this sudden and unlooked-for interruption, raised their heads and faced the infuriated intruders, who glared fiercely at them, and smote their cutlasses with vehemence on the deck.

Pausing upon the threshold, the buccaneers surveyed the features of the alarmed and terrified females, in the endeavour to trace the signs of guilt upon the faces of one or both of them.

"Where is the traitress?" they shouted, in a breath.

"Not here. Back—back!" cried one of the ladies, in a firm, commanding voice, as she checked their advance with a movement of her outstretched hand.

It was Mrs. Drake who spoke.

She had drawn her queenly form erect and to its full height, and Minnie, with a fluttering heart, nestled to her womanly breast for protection.

This, by the rage-blinded buccaneers, was naturally construed to be a sign of Minnie's guilt.

"Forward! Seize the traitress," cried one of men whose head was swathed in a blood-stained bandage. "Give her no quarter! Death—death!"

Incited by this fiercely-uttered cry, the rest of the buccaneers pressed forward, and with gleaming eyes and still deadlier gleaming cutlasses prepared to cut the young girl down.

But at this moment, so fraught with peril to the young affianced bride, a well-known voice smote the ears of the would-be assailants, causing each one to instinctively pause, paralysed, as it were, with fear, and Admiral Tom Drake, dashing through their midst, leapt to the side of his betrothed.

To encircle her delicate waist with his strong and sinewy arm and whisper a few cheering words in her ear was to Tom but the work of a moment, and then, as his bright sword leapt like a flash of lightning from its sheath, he faced her would-be destroyers.

"Hounds! merciless wolves!" Admiral Tom shouted, "why are you here? By whose and what authority do you dare venture upon this intrusion?"

Awed by his presence the buccaneers drew back, but not one of them had the courage to reply.

Tom's eyes now fairly blazed, and seemed to vie in dazzling brightness with the sparkling jewels that decked the hilt of his sword.

He paused a few seconds to ascertain whether any of the men would muster up courage enough to speak, but all were silent, and the admiral again commenced.

"Fools, knaves that you are," he indignantly exclaimed, "were you not the victim of some cruel and fiendish deceit, I would strike you lifeless at my feet, stretch you as so many stark and gory corps on this snowy deck, which you have dared to pollute with your unholy tread. But I pity you," he added, his cheeks now all aglow, and his eyes flashing, if possible, with greater brilliancy. "That my sweet Minnie is entirely innocent of the foul aspersion cast upon her shall be fully proved, for the bride of Admiral Tom Drake must not dwell even under the shadow of such an awful suspicion."

A slight movement and a subdued murmur amongst the men told that Tom's speech was well received, and that his promise had renewed their faith in Minnie Atherton.

One of them appeared about to speak, but Admiral Tom cared not to hold further converse with them just then.

Motioning them to depart, he closed the door with the point of his sword, and then directed his attention to his beloved Minnie, who, overcome by the excitement, had swooned.

* * * * * *

Two days have passed. The strict routine and discipline pursued on board the "Will-o'-the-Wisp" was restored and maintained without any hitch or disturbance.

Great changes have, however, been wrought on board Tom Drake's tight little vessel.

Rais Hassan had been returned to his cell, which, being lined inside with sheet iron, was thus rendered impregnable to the flames, and Jacop was placed under close arrest between a couple of spare guns, which were lashed on the main deck for handiness and security.

But Jacop, although deprived of his office and placed in durance vile, had not divulged one sentence to incriminate himself, nor to excite suspicion that he was in collusion with the Corsair maiden, Zelie.

Far from it. He stuck to his original story, and, to all threats and promises that were used to shake his testimony, his only reply was that he was being slowly murdered, and that when he was dead and gone they would find out that he was a martyr.

Mickey, the marine, however, paid dearly for his perfidy.

The drugged spirits and the smoke put an untimely end to his career, for he neither rallied nor spoke after he was conveyed on deck, and he was cast into the sea, unpitied, unwept for, and not even regretted, unless it was for the reason that he had not lived long enough to have confessed his complicity in the incendiary crime.

Under such circumstances Zelie was comparatively safe, though she was unhappy, for her plot had failed, and Minnie had been adjudged innocent by the whole of the crew.

But there were three on board who were more anxious than the rest put together to learn the truth and have the mystery cleared up. They were Admiral Tom, Ben Barnacle, and Harry Vere.

All three, both together and separately, had visited the Corsair chief in his incarceration, but failed to elicit any tangible information from him; and as he, chafing under his captivity, no doubt, gradually subsided into a dogged and sullen silence on the matter, they resolved to let him rest for a time.

Admiral Tom, during all this, never relaxed his vigilance in looking after the safety of his ship and the valuable prize she had in tow, and his watchful eye was kept ever on the alert, for strange vessels were continually flitting about upon the horizon, and the news he gleaned from the ships he spoke with gave him notice that the Spaniards, as well as the French, were cruising the seas like so many hungry sharks.

It was this that served to break the dull monotony of the voyage, which was certainly tedious to the restless admiral.

When the wind fell light the progress of the convoy was scarcely perceptible, so that when the lofty peak of the rock of Gibraltar was descried it was hailed with joy.

Bob and Jerry, just previous to the cheering hail, were below, both being seated on the deck, the former with a meat kid upon his knees, in which was a piece of boiled salt pork, and the latter with a kid of pea-soup steadied between his outspread legs, from which imprisonment it seemed determined to escape at every roll and lurch of the ship.

"This is pea-soup with a vengeance," Jerry was saying, as with a large wooden spoon he bailed up some of the coloured, or rather discoloured, greasy water. "Why, the peas are as hard as bullets, and the duff's as tough as pump-leather. Whew! one needs the teeth and digestion of a halligator to get it into one."

"You're no worse off than me," echoed Bob, casting his eyes up dolefully. "I wish we was at the 'Yaller Halligator,' for this pork's as hard as the sheave of a tops'l-sheet block; there's nothing of it but a piece of hard rind, about four inches or so of shrivelled-up wood, and a bone as big as our Admiral's cocked hat."

"Sarves us right, Bob; we shouldn't 'a been sailors. You see, them as stays ashore has their wives, and such like, to cook for them properly, whilst us tars has to put up with hard knocks, hard biscuits, and hard weather, and with hard—ly any meat."

"That's very good, Jerry, if you aren't inclined to be funny; but I'll make up for all this when I get ashore. I'll order a dozen of everything from a broiled fowl to a roasted helephant."

"And soup as well?"

"In course, but not grape-shot and cannister boiled in greasy water like what you're nussing there as if it was pap for a blessed baby. Hullo! what's that horrid smell? Somebody's stirring up the bilge-water?"

The worthy pair took a couple of extra sniffs, and then eyed each other with dejected mien and terribly hungry-looking glances.

The cook's mate at that moment had passed along the deck with a tureen of steaming turtle soup, which scented the air with its savoury aroma, and which was delightfully wafted down the hatchway, and set the stomachs of the two hungry and disgusted tars grumbling.

"Oh, crikey!" Jerry Mizzen suddenly exclaimed, as he clasped both hands over the buckle of his belt, "wouldn't I just like to let out a reef or two and take in a cargo of that horrid beastly stuff!"

Bob tried to laugh, but his features were not flexible enough to perform the operation.

"Would you like it served out to you in the water cask or the long boat?" he asked, drily

"Oh! the long boat, just about level up to the thwarts, would do."

"And would you like any pertickler appliance to bail it out with?"

"A couple of buckets 'ud serve me, one down and t'other come on; but I'd like to have it ashore, you know, because if the ship chanced to roll much a pint or more of it might get capsized, and I shouldn't like to lose a drop. You see, Bob?"

"In course not," Bob replied, as he caught the mischievous twinkle of his eye. "But hadn't we better go in for some of this just to lay a sort of groundwork like? You'd need a little dunnage, you know, to stow a precious cargo like that upon."

"That's a happy thought," said Jerry, suddenly brightening up. "We shall be called on deck directly, and then we shan't get none."

And this happened rather earlier than they anticipated.

The cry of "Land oh, oh, oh!" from the masthead caused them both to spring to their feet, and Bob's legs, getting ontangled with the meat kid, compelled him to spin round, whilst his foot, alighting on the abused piece of pork, caused him to trip, and eventually seat himself with a flop in the vessel containing the pea-soup.

Jerry Mizzen burst into a roar of boisterous laughter.

"You're safe moored now," he said. "Shall I lend you a hand to get out, or let you rest there while I take the bearings of the land, shipmate?"

"Give me a heave-up, of course, you lubber. I'm as fast as a rock and my back's nearly twisted in halves, you grinning hyæna."

Bob roared out this.

He was not only annoyed at Jerry's mirth, but also at the helpless predicament he found himself in, for his nether portions fitted so accurately into the rims of the pea-soup kid that one might well have been compared to a cork and the other to the neck of a huge pickling-jar.

But a commotion on deck soon put an end to this fun.

Jerry, getting behind him, caught him beneath the armpits and, jerking him on to his feet, sprang up the hatchway, leaving him to follow at will.

Bob Hauler did not tarry a moment, but on reaching the deck he wished he had tarried below just for one moment so as to give himself a brush-down, for his presence was greeted by a loud "Haw! haw!" from a group of middies collected near the hatchway, which made Bob decidedly savage.

His white canvas pants were not only discoloured with the soup, but were spangled all over the seat with the crushed peas, upon which he had so unceremoniously sat.

When land was sighted Admiral Tom evinced more anxiety than he had hitherto displayed.

The spyglass, when not at his eye, was either tucked under his arm ready for instant use, or used by him to point out distant objects to the ladies assembled on the quarter-deck.

Tables loaded with rich wines and savoury biscuits were placed at intervals so as to allow of each party enjoying one another's society separately, and nothing conducive to comfort was wanting or had been overlooked.

Suddenly the admiral whispered the order for these to be cleared away.

"Show the ladies below," he said to his young lieutenant, Harry Vere. "Ask no questions," he added, as Harry glanced inquiringly into his face; "there is a big ship rounding the point yonder, and she may wish to speak us!"

Harry Vere quite understood what the admiral's meaning glance was intended to convey.

As his quick eye glanced towards the point of land, from which the tall sails and masts of the strange vessel were rapidly opening, he could make out that she was a frigate of no ordinary size.

"A Spaniard, by old Neptune!" exclaimed Harry, as he returned on deck from handing the last of his fair charges below, "and she bristles with guns, too, as I can see by her half-raised ports!"

"Let her come on, then!" said old Ben Barnacle, grimly. "There's ne'er a Spaniard afloat that we need care for. Shall I signal to the prizes, admiral, and pass the word to prepare?"

"Aye—aye—do so!" cried Admiral Tom, excitedly. "Prepare for action! Prepare to give them a sound drubbing! Prepare for another well-earned victory, for I sight another of the rascals in the first one's wake, and I have no doubt they mean to intercept us."

"And capture us and our prizes!" said Harry Vere, with a light-hearted laugh, as he buckled on his cutlass and stuck a couple of boarding pistols in his belt.

Then he leaped forward among the men, who

in quietness, but with promptitude and precision, cut loose the broadside guns, prepared the handspikes, rammers, and shot, and emptied the arm-chests of pistols, cutlasses, boarding-pikes, and tomahawks.

As the action was likely to be a severe one, Jenny Vere and Zelie were armed with pistols and dirks, and Mrs. Drake and Mrs. Harpy were furnished with long stilettos, with which to protect themselves from insult in the event of the " Will-o'-the-Wisp" being boarded.

No one on board dreamt of such an event, and Admiral Tom laughed the idea to scorn; but, as he observed when he issued the order, and gave his mother an assuring kiss, it was as well to be prepared in case of accidents.

This proved true.

In less than an hour the two formidable ships hoisted Spanish colours, and, without even hailing the " Will-o'-the-Wisp," they each poured a broadside point blank into her.

" Show them our flag, Barnacle," said Admiral Tom, as with flashing eye and quivering lip he beheld the splinters fly from the stout sides of his dear old ship.

Ben ran the old fly aloft.

" They know us," he said, " already. That treacherous volley was meant to disable us, and——"

" Let them have it!" cried Admiral Tom, " Ready there, fore and aft. I hope every gun is double-shotted."

" Aye, aye, admiral!" was Harry Vere's reply, " and our prize frigate has obeyed the same order. The iron chestnuts are nearly roasted too, admiral."

Admiral Tom seized his speaking trumpet and sprang on to the signal-chest, and then his clarion-like voice rang out, and the battle was begun in earnest.

Hampered by the vessels he had in tow, Admiral Tom, but for his superior gunnery, would have lost the day, as the Spanish men-of-war outmanœuvred him on every tack.

The largest of the Spanish vessels—a two-decker, carrying an armament almost double to that of the " Will-o'-the-Wisp," and commanded by Admiral Bonaventura More s, the same who was rear-admiral over the formidable floating batteries that took part in the siege of Gibralter a few years previous to the date of the action we now record poured such showers of iron into the ribs of the sturdy little " Will-o'-the-Wisp" as to cause Admiral Tom at such times to concentrate all his armament upon her.

The smaller vessel—the " San Juan," commanded by Don Pablo de Oosa—paid attention more especially to the English prize frigate and the Barbary corsair, among which two vessels, with a few of Admiral Tom's own men to officer them, the crew of the English frigate was distributed.

For three long hours this unequal and memorable action was maintained, the saucy " Will-o'-the-Wisp" during that space having effectually dismounted nearly the whole of the enemy's guns, fired their ships in a score of places with red-hot shot, and finally dismasted the big two-decker.

Admiral Tom's ship was almost a wreck.

The water poured through numerous shot-holes in her sides, the carpenter, aided by his mates, being unable to provide shot plugs and drive them in fast enough; her sails and rigging hung in shreds and tatters.

It was exactly as the hour-glass was turned,

and the bell of the " Will-o'-the-Wisp" pronounced that the last dog watch was up, when the tide of battle turned in our hero's favour.

Admiral Bonaventura Morens struck his flag. His boats, being hastily got afloat and crowded with men, were pulled towards the San Juan.

A great many of the Spanish seamen then jumped overboard, and clung to the spars which dotted the sea.

Then a loud huzza burst from the English throats.

The victory was theirs, and as the Spanish admiral's flag-ship broke out in one sheet of lambent flame, Ben Barnacle, Harry Vere, and half a dozen of the middies clambered up the splintered and shot-battered side of the " Will-o'-the-Wisp."

Their temporary absence had not been noticed in the excitement that prevailed, so that when they leaped upon the deck and Harry waved the Spanish flag above his head a deafening British cheer welcomed their return.

" Hurrah!—hurrah!" yelled Bob and Jerry. " Hurrah for our gallant officers, Ben Barnacle and Harry Vere!"

*　*　*　*　*　*

Days have passed.

Admiral Tom went below to personally interrogate the prisoner Jacop, who had been placed out of shot-range during the action, and was now about to undergo his trial by court-martial.

The admiral was alone, and as he descended to the deck on which Jacop was confined the sound of voices in angry altercation caused him to cautiously proceed, when, to his surprise, he beheld Zelie and the late captain of the cockpit engaged in what appeared to be a deadly struggle.

And such it proved, for the wiry Jacop had already got one hand on the throat of the corsair maiden, whilst with the other hand, in which he grasped an iron belaying-pin, he smashed in the Arabian girl's face, and she fell dead and bleeding on the deck.

Admiral Tom Drake stood for some seconds petrified with horror.

He could scarcely believe his eyesight, and especially when he saw Jacop bend down to the deck and snatch up from the fresh-made pool of gore the very diamond, the big sea emerald, for which our hero had risked so much, and of which he had so mysteriously lost possession.

To leap forward and snatch it from the hand of the maniacal boy, who, with the fatal lustre irradiating his distorted visage, was gloating over its sparkling brilliancy, was his first impulsive movement; but his foot slipping on the wet, slippery deck apprised Jacop of his intention, and, with the yell of a savage Indian, he leaped up the hatchway on to the upper deck, and, springing through an open gunport, plunged into the sea.

" Lower a boat—lower a boat!" shrieked Admiral Tom, his eyes ready to start from his head.

But it was too late.

As the boy's head rose to the surface of the water a huge shark made its appearance, there was a sickening crash, a soul-rending shriek, and then the shark, Jacop, and the big sea emerald disappeared beneath the blood tinged waves for ever.

*　*　*　*　*　*

Portsmouth Harbour.

How the gay bunting flies from the flagstaffs

on shore, the fort, the battery, the admiral's house, and even the coastguard station.

And how the shipping is decked with streamers, whilst salvoes of cannon add life to the scene, and announce that some great event is about to take place.

Admiral Tom Drake, with his shot-battered "Will-o'-the-Wisp," has arrived, his victorious battle flag flaunting defiantly in the wind, his two prizes still in tow, and his bright guns belching forth flame and smoke in answer to the welcome salute that greets him on all sides.

At the wheel of one of the prizes, rendered conspicuous by a long pigtail plaited neatly into his own hair and allowed to fall gracefully down between his shoulders, is Bob Hauler; while on the other prize Jerry Mizzen performs a similar duty, and rejoices in the same time-honoured decoration.

The men-of-war forming a guard of honour are a squadron detached from the Channel fleet on purpose to meet Admiral Tom and convey him and his prizes safely home as soon as the news of his glorious achievements reached the Admiralty.

As soon as the ships came to anchor the Port-Admiral, in his gold-laced uniform and cocked hat, boarded the "Will-o'-the-Wisp" in his barge, and, in the presence of those who surrounded the young commander, there and then presented him with a packet, containing his full pardon, and a royal letter granting him restitution of his national rights and privileges, both of which bore the signature and seal of his Britannic Majesty King George.

At the same time a boat with Post-Captain Portsill and a guard of marines on board rowed to the "Will-o'-the-Wisp," and, without allowing Ben Barnacle time to remove his pigtail, which he had spliced with seaman-like neatness to his silvered locks, or Harry Vere to change the true blue uniform of the British navy, which he had donned as a mark of respect to the squadron that had guarded them safely up channel, conveyed them on board the guard-ship.

Having been ushered into the cabin of the Flag Admiral, who was at the time comparing the notes in his log-book with some documentary evidence, which was written on parchment, the deeds past and present of our two worthy friends were discussed, reviewed, and severely commented upon, which resulted, owing to the intercession of Post-Captain Portsill, in the Admiral promising to forward a good report of them to the proper quarter, where he had not the slightest doubt that the capture of the Spanish flag would not only be looked upon as an act of heroism, but one that would entitle them to a free pardon and a commission in his Majesty's navy, by which means they could ascend the ladder of promotion and fame.

*　　*　　*　　*

In the meantime the conduct of Admiral Ellis was severely censured, but, for all that, preparations were made to effect a change of prisoners, which in the end resulted in the liberation of Rais Hassan and the return to England of Admiral Ellis.

Of Lord Kilcrew and Lieutenant Gaston we cannot speak so favourably. They lost their heads through making too free with the ladies in the harem attached to the palace of the Bey, and thus they fell victims to their own rashness and cupidity within the walls of Algiers.

And so time wore on until one bright morning the marriage bells rang merrily and Admiral Tom Drake, escorted by his old friends and the *élite* of the society in which Tom at various periods of his adventurous life moved, led his beauteous and blushing bride to the altar.

Lords were there; ladies who boasted beauty, wealth, and title were the bridesmaids; and in the gay *cortege* escutcheons blazed in the golden sunlight, and the richly-caparisoned horses seemed to share in the glory of the day.

Lady Arbuthnot and Lady Castlemaine were prominent in the brilliant assemblage, and so were Harry and Jenny Vere.

Also Bob Hauler and Jerry Mizzen, the former bearing a massive silver anchor upon his shoulder, and the latter carrying the battle flag of Admiral Tom Drake on a long, gilded staff.

Old John Gregory, likewise Mrs. Harpy, were among the anxious throng, while old Ben Barnacle, who proved to be our hero's father, supported the tottering steps of his wife, and led her to a seat provided for her near the altar.

All was joy. The nuptial ceremony was soon concluded, and then the merry bells again pealed, rustics shouted till they were hoarse, and the brilliant equipages rolled on towards the ancestral hall of the Athertons, Admiral Tom Drake and his peerless bride being seated together in their carriage, the equipment of which, and the caparisons of their horses, were rich in gold and sparkling jewels.

We have little to add now.

When Doctor Birchenhall, who had been a sad and silent witness of the marriage, returned to his establishment, he found that the guilty Sanderson was dead; but whether he died of any violent action of his own, or was visited by the just retribution that attends the wrongdoer, was never divulged.

Admiral Ellis arrived in England broken down by disgrace and imprisonment, and died soon after broken-hearted, but not before he had sought and obtained forgiveness of his daughter Jenny and his son-in-law.

Strange to relate, on the wedding evening the "Blue Lobster" was blown up, and the "Yellow Alligator" the next day was set fire to by some drunken brawlers, and the iniquitous den was razed to the ground.

A week later the "Will-o'-the-Wisp" was placed in dock to undergo repairs, and when her costly treasures were removed to a place of safety, and her guns and stores taken out, a startling discovery was made.

In a secret nook in the lower hold a package of letters was found, and rolled up with them was a valuable jewelled star, which Captain Tom recognised at once as having been worn Zelie.

The signature of the writer of the letters was that of Mickey the marine's deserted wife; so that Admiral Tom, who secretly believed that Zelie and the marine were in some way connected with the attempted firing of the ship, now had no doubt that the pair were guilty, and he fervently thanked heaven for having chastised them in its own inscrutable way.

And thus, dear readers, the adventures of Admiral—once Captain—Tom Drake and his middies, old England's true hearts of oak, are brought to a close.

THE END.

www.ingramcontent.com/pod-product-compliance
Lightning Source LLC
Chambersburg PA
CBHW082053220626
47052CB00006B/1224